J6781170332

THE MYSTERY
OF THE WOODEN LEGS
&
SEVEN WHITE PEBBLES

The Mystery of the Wooden Legs

GRISELDA GIFFORD

Illustrated by Barry Wilkinson

Seven White Pebbles

HELEN CLARE

Illustrated by Cynthia Abbott

NEW ACORN LIBRARY

THE BODLEY HEAD

LONDON · SYDNEY TORONTO

© Griselda Gifford 1964 and © Helen Clare 1960
Illustrations © The Bodley Head Ltd 1964 and 1960
ISBN 0 370 11000 5
Printed in Great Britain for
The Bodley Head Ltd
9 Bow Street, London WC2E 7AL
by BAS Printers Ltd, Wallop, Hampshire
Set in Monophoto Plantin
This edition first published 1975

The Mystery of the Wooden Legs was first published
in the Bodley Head Acorn Library in 1964,
and *Seven White Pebbles* in 1960.

CONTENTS

The Mystery
of the Wooden Legs

GRISELDA GIFFORD

Illustrated by Barry Wilkinson

I

Sue was trying very hard to whistle, as she stared out of the window, but although she puffed and blew, nothing happened. She wished she and her mother were back in the cottage in the country, with Tiddles, their cat, but her mother said it cost too much to live there, and it was too far from the hospital where she worked as a nurse.

They were not allowed to keep animals in their flat, which was a basement. All Sue could see out of the window were two dustbins, a stone wall with railings at the top and the steps leading up into the street. Someone walked past, with a click-click of high heels, but Sue had to guess what she looked like from the shoes, for she could see no higher.

A pair of stout, lace-up shoes marched past. Miss Wilkinson, who lived in one room at the top of the house, was going to her work at the Post Office. Black high heels tripped past next, and the shoes had a gay little bow in front. Sue had never seen their owner, who came past every morning, but she imagined someone with swinging fair hair and gay clothes.

Mr Hyde's old but well-polished shoes came past; he was easy to recognise because he had a slight limp. She thought he was probably very brave in the war, and had been wounded. He also had a room in the house, and stuttered 'Gggood morning,' when they met him emptying his rubbish into the dustbin on Sunday. Very probably he was frightened of meeting Mrs Mudge, their grumpy landlady.

Sue was just wondering whether to get her three old dolls out and play hospitals, when she saw something very odd. Two sticks were walking along the pavement, one after the other, just like legs. And behind the sticks were four furry paws and behind them, the red wheels of a tricycle and two small feet wearing very dirty sandals, firmly on the ground as their owner had obviously not learned to use the pedals yet. Then Sue saw a thin piece of rope hanging down behind the tricycle and nearly touching the pavement. The rope twitched a little at the tip!

As quickly as possible, she rushed out of the flat and up the steps, but she was too late. The street was empty, and as grey and dull as it always was. The owners of the paws, the sticks, the wheels and

the 'rope' must have turned the corner, and Sue was not allowed outside the door on her own. She looked at the sooty trees in the gardens in the middle of the square, and envied the lucky children who were allowed to play there.

'Sue!' called her mother. 'Come in, dear.'

She went inside the flat. Her mother was wearing a blue dressing-gown and her face was red and creased on one side, where she had lain on it. 'I asked you not to go outside when I'm asleep,' she said.

'Sorry,' said Sue. 'But I saw something very peculiar outside.'

'Oh, yes, dear,' said Mrs Smith, yawning, and she went into the kitchen to put the kettle on.

'Couldn't we have a key to the gardens?' Sue asked, following her mother and sitting down on the bath, because the kitchen was a bathroom, too. Sue had suggested once that it would be rather fun to eat breakfast in the bath.

'I've told you, Mrs Mudge won't lend us her key, and only people who own houses in the square can have a key of their own,' Mrs Smith said. 'After all, you have the garden at the back to play in,' she added in her brisk, making-the-best-of-it voice.

'But it's so small and unsunny,' said Sue. 'I don't like the town. At home the daffodils and primroses would be out now.' She still thought of the cottage as home.

Mrs Smith made her tea. 'It's much easier for me, here,' she said. 'Now I'm near the hospital I can get back to you quickly after my night's work, and have a longer sleep, too. We'll go out shopping when I've dressed. It's lovely to have the shops so near.'

'I wish you didn't have to go out to work,' Sue said. 'Nursing makes you so tired and you've never got time to go for walks.'

'We need the money,' said Sue's mother. 'And I love nursing. But I miss our walks in the country, too.'

Sue thought about the time when Daddy was alive. Her mother just looked after their dear little cottage, then, and had plenty of time to cook and give tea-parties for Sue's friends, and she always seemed to be laughing. Now, she looked sad quite often, and although she was a cheerful person, her laughter wasn't the same.

When Sue and her mother went out of the door, carrying shopping-baskets, they saw Mrs Mudge's kitchen door opening slowly, and Mrs Mudge peeped through the crack. 'If you're going shopping, I'd be glad of a few potatoes,' she said. 'Can't get about like I used to.'

Mrs Smith sighed. 'All right, Mrs Mudge. How many pounds?'

'Five would keep me going a few days,' said Mrs Mudge. She ate a great deal and seemed to get fatter every day. 'Miss Wilkinson said she heard *singing* the other evening,' she went on. 'You know I don't usually have children in my house. I have to think of my tenants.'

'But I was only singing in the garden,' Sue said. 'Quite a nice song, too. *Cherry Ripe.* I learned it at school last term.'

'Miss Wilkinson can hear every sound from the garden,' said Mrs Mudge, with an angry frown.

'But . . .' Sue began crossly.

'I'm sure Sue will be quiet in future,' said her mother. 'I'll get the potatoes for you, Mrs Mudge.'

Mrs Mudge grunted, and shut her door.

'Oh, she's awful,' said Sue as they went up the steps. 'And it's not fair. I wasn't singing loudly and we've got enough to carry without her beastly old potatoes. Yesterday it was turnips. She's strong. I saw her carrying a great big rug under her arm one day, along the street. I expect she'd been pushing people around at a sale to get it.'

'We just have to keep her happy,' said her mother. 'I had to persuade her very hard to take us, and it isn't easy to find cheap flats where they take children. Come on, let's forget about Mrs Mudge. It's a lovely day.'

It was a lovely day, and even here, in the centre of the town, you could smell the scent of spring, and all the sparrows were twittering as they made their nests in the square garden and among the roofs and chimney-pots. Sue jumped over a puddle and felt happy.

They went out into the street market, and passed stalls heaped with shiny oranges and bunches of bananas like fat yellow fingers; stalls heaped with purple cabbages, red and green apples and cascades of grapes, and stalls smothered in rolls of material or piled high with beads and necklaces. Sue liked the market, but today she hardly noticed anything because she was too busy looking for someone with wooden legs, followed by a large furry thing, followed by a child on a tricycle with *something* hanging down, perhaps a rope?

But they saw nothing unusual, and after lunch Sue helped her mother with the housework. Afterwards, Mrs Smith went to have another sleep, because, as she said, it was no good being a tired nurse. Sue went into the back garden, which was enclosed by high walls. On either side were houses, in a long terrace, and the back of another terrace cut out the sunshine beyond the bottom wall. Nothing grew in the garden, except ivy and some very sick-looking weeds.

Sue looked to see if some marigold seeds, planted when they first arrived, had come up, but the sooty earth was bare. Then she brought out her three dolls and practised bandaging their legs and arms because she was going to be a nurse, too.

At tea, her mother said, 'Cheer up. You'll be starting your new school before very long.'

'I liked the old one,' said Sue.

'You'll never make a good nurse if you're so gloomy,' her mother said. 'I know. We'll have chocolate biscuits for a treat and then we'll play *Snap*.'

Very soon, too soon, it was bed-time, and Sue's mother kissed her good-night before going to the hospital. The bedroom door was always left open,

and Sue could see through the sitting-room into the hall, where the light was on, although it wasn't yet dark. On the other side of the hall was Mrs Mudge's kitchen, where she always sat in the evenings because she kept her front room, upstairs, for special occasions. In a little while, Mrs Mudge would come into the hall and stand in the doorway, looking like a great black teacosy against the light, with her head for the knob of the teapot. Sue always breathed loudly, as if she were asleep, because once a nightmare had made her call out and Mrs Mudge had come into the room and leaned over her, smelling of onions and moth-balls, which was much worse than the nightmare.

Mrs Mudge went away, and Sue thought about the queer procession she had seen out of the window. Who could they be? She must find out.

2

The next morning, Sue watched out of the window for a long time. She thought: 'How silly I am. They may never come this way again,' and grew rather bored. Suddenly, she saw the wooden legs, followed by the furry paws, and without waiting for the tricycle she shot out of the front door and up the steps, just in time to see a very small boy on a red tricycle. A little black monkey sat on his back and its long tail nearly touched the pavement.

But the rest of the procession had just turned the corner, and the little boy, using his feet to get along, was out of sight in a minute. At that moment, Mrs Smith's alarm clock rang loudly and Sue hurried back.

All day she thought about the boy and his strange friends and hoped very hard she would see them again.

Sure enough, the very next morning the wooden sticks marched past the window! This time, Sue ran out immediately, but all she saw was the boy on his tricycle. 'Do stop!' she called, and ran down the street after him, but he turned the corner and an angry voice called: 'Susan! Come back at once! I shall tell your mother!'

She stopped and looked back. Mrs Mudge stood on the front doorstep, red-faced and frowning.

Sue hurried back. 'Don't wake Mummy!' she called anxiously. Her mother was always so tired after working all night.

'Running wild in the streets,' Mrs Mudge said

when Sue came in. 'I'll certainly tell your mother right away.'

So poor Mrs Smith was woken up twenty minutes before her alarm went (the procession was early this morning) by Mrs Mudge banging on the door.

'Found her in the street,' Mrs Mudge said. 'Not to be trusted. Running off on her own like that.'

'Thank you for calling her back,' Mrs Smith said, and when Sue was inside and Mrs Mudge the other side of the door, she went on, 'Sue, dear, I know it's boring having nobody to play with. But I really can't have you playing in the street alone. You might go off exploring and get lost.'

'I've seen children younger than me playing in the street,' Sue said. 'After all, I'm seven.'

'You're not used to traffic,' said Mrs Smith. 'Perhaps later on, when you've some schoolfriends to play with and when you know the town better.'

So Sue promised not to go in the street again. Now she would never know who had wooden legs, or who owned the furry paws, unless she just happened to meet them in the street when they were out shopping.

The following day, she couldn't help looking out

for the procession again. But she waited and waited, and again it was a lovely day, and she lost interest now she couldn't go outside and find out who the odd people were. She went into the back garden and wondered what to do.

She looked at the wall that divided the end of their garden from the little gardens at the back of the other row of terrace houses, and had an idea. If she climbed up, standing on an old box someone had left in the corner, she could sit on the top. Perhaps the garden on the other side would be interesting?

It was rather a scramble but she reached the top, only to be disappointed. The other garden was just as small and dark as hers, and there was nobody to talk to.

Sue had another good idea. She would walk right along the wall, between the little back gardens. Nobody would mind, and she might see some children or have an adventure.

When she stood up, she felt a long way from the ground, but she had done plenty of tree-climbing in the country, and the wall was broad, so she walked quite easily.

As it was such a fine day, everyone had hung

their washing out, and she enjoyed guessing who lived in the houses as she went along. Next door but one from their house was a line hung with nappies and a pram in the garden, and the garden after that, on the right-hand side of the wall, had a row of very darned clothes. Then, further down, again on her right, seven pairs of striped pyjamas danced on the line. They went down in sizes to a very small pair, so she guessed there were seven boys living there, or perhaps a father and six sons —and the mother who did the washing. How did they all fit into that narrow house? She rather hoped nobody grown up would see her, because they might ask what she was doing, but it was a pity there were no children in the gardens.

Perhaps if she went a little further . . . Suddenly she heard a sort of growl; not the sort of growl a dog makes but a noise that reminded her of the Zoo. She looked down into the garden on her right and gave a start of surprise. Crouched on a pile of old newspapers was an enormous cat! No, it had yellow eyes, a golden coat and a long tail that was waving angrily. It was a lion cub! Beyond the cub was the little boy with the tricycle, walking it round and round in a circle, with the monkey on his shoulder.

'Is that your lion?' she asked him.

He looked up, pulled a toy pistol out of his pocket and pointed it at her. 'Go away!' he shouted and the pistol went off, bang! so loudly that she nearly fell off the wall.

The cub growled. 'Eat her up! Eat her up!' shouted the small boy. Sue wondered if cubs could climb walls, and decided not to wait to find out.

It seemed a long way back as the wall was not broad enough to run along and she was still rather frightened by the growling.

While she was reaching for the box with her feet, her mother called, 'Sue!' from the kitchen door.

'Here,' Sue called back.

'Mrs Mudge or one of the neighbours might see you,' her mother said in a worried voice. 'I came out to look for you and you weren't there. Don't walk along the wall again, Sue. I'm sure people won't like it, and I don't know where you've got to.'

The rest of the morning Sue was miserable because she had forgotten how scared she had been of the lion cub, and she wanted to go back along the wall and see if the man with the wooden legs came into the garden with the boy and the monkey and the lion cub. Now it looked as if she would never see what he looked like.

3

Two days later, though, something exciting happened. When Mrs Smith woke up, she asked Sue to bring in the milk from the top of the step, and there they were!

But there was no man with wooden legs. In front was a boy of about her own age, walking on high wooden stilts, and behind him came the lion cub, on a lead, and behind the cub were the little boy and the monkey, on the tricycle.

It was now or never. 'Oh, please could I try your stilts?' she called out, because it was something she had always wanted to do.

The boy looked surprised, and then he frowned. He had a fringe of black hair that almost went into his eyes and made him look like a cross Yorkshire terrier. '*You'd* be no good,' he said scornfully, and walked on. The little boy brought out his gun and fired it.

'Go away!' he shouted.

'Where's the milk?' called Sue's mother. 'I want my cup of tea!'

And at the same moment, Mrs Mudge came puffing up the steps. She saw the two boys and her face went a mottled red. 'Gypsy children! And in the square! Go away, at once! Oh . . . is that a . . .? No, it can't be. Yes, it is! A lion!' She seized Susan's arm and pulled her down the steps and indoors. 'A lion cub! Think of the danger! I'll ring the Police! Mrs Smith!'

Sue's mother came to the door, heavy with sleep. 'Good morning, Mrs Mudge,' she said.

'You should keep your eye on Susan!' shouted Mrs Mudge. 'This is the second time I've caught her. She'd have been after two gypsy boys and their dangerous dirty animals if I hadn't come along.'

'Come in, Sue,' said Mrs Smith. 'I'm sure she wouldn't have followed the boys, Mrs Mudge, because she knows now she mustn't go in the street. Goodbye,' and she closed the door gently but firmly.

'What was she talking about?' Sue's mother asked.

Sue told her about the lion, the little boy and the monkey, and the larger boy on stilts.

'Are you sure it was a lion cub? I don't think

they'd be able to take it round the streets like that,' said Mrs Smith, as she poured out her tea. 'Perhaps it was a lionish sort of dog.'

Sue was going to argue and then she thought it would be rather nice to keep the lion to herself, especially as she might never really get to know it. Then she could make up stories about the animals and the boys when she was in bed and feeling lonely.

She sipped her own tea, which was the colour of pale gold, because they always had the top of the milk 'to give ourselves a treat in the morning,' as her mother said. At teatime, Sue had to drink milk. She felt a little bit guilty. 'I wanted to try his stilts in the street but he wouldn't let me,' she admitted.

'Just as well,' said Mrs Smith. 'And it was a bit silly of you as I'd asked you not to play in the street. I wouldn't mind so much if I was awake and if I could see you out of the window . . .'

'Sorry,' said Sue, and the rest of the day she tried to be extra good, and her mother was specially cheerful, too, but all the time Sue thought sadly of the boys. She had so much wanted to make friends with them.

The next day, Sue and her mother were in the market after lunch, looking for a cabbage 'with a really good heart,' Mrs Smith said, when Sue heard someone crying.

The man with the banana stall shouted, 'Lovely naarnaas,' and Sue couldn't hear the crying, but she slipped away from her mother and looked round. If only she were a bit bigger, she thought as she tried to see round the jostling people, who towered over her like tall trees. She heard the crying again, looked behind a pile of boxes, and saw the little boy, who was still sitting on his red tricycle.

'What's the matter?' she asked.

'Want Gan,' he sobbed. The monkey's black eyes looked frightened and it clung to the boy's shoulders.

'Where do you live?' Sue asked him. Of course, she had seen the back of his house, but she had no idea which number it was from the street, and in fact she had never been along that road, behind her own home.

'Want Gan, want Gan, want Dan, want Dan,' he answered, which was rather confusing.

'I'll find them for you,' she said. 'Come along.' She tried to push the tricycle, but he went very red in the face and shouted, 'No, No!'

'Can't you pedal it?' she asked as he followed her, walking it along as usual, but he didn't answer.

'What's wrong?' Sue's mother asked, when she saw him.

'Lost,' said Sue.

'Poor little thing, and that tiny monkey, too! He must be one of the boys you saw the other day.' Mrs Smith gave him a jelly baby from the packet she had just bought, but the monkey snatched it and ate it up in three bites, so the boy had to be given another one. 'What's your name?' Mrs Smith asked him.

The little boy said something that sounded like 'Cocoa' but the sweet rather got in the way.

'Do you know where you live?' Sue's mother asked him.

'Want Gan, want Dan,' was all Cocoa would say.

'We'd better take him to the Police Station.' Mrs Smith looked worried.

'I think I can find his home,' said Sue. 'I saw him the day I walked along the wall. It was a house on my . . . on my right, so it's in a street behind the square.'

'We could go down the street behind our house,' said her mother. 'You probably won't remember how far down the house is, but he'll remember his own home.'

To reach the road where Cocoa lived, they had to cross the square, and by the time they were passing their own house, Cocoa stopped walking his tricycle along and began to cry again. 'Want Dan!' he bawled with his mouth square, like a letter-box.

Sue tried to get him to go on, but he screamed, 'Want Dan! Want to be carried!'

Sue's mother picked him up with the little monkey still clinging to his shoulders. 'Goodness, he's heavy,' she said. 'And he can't be much more than two years old. I hope the monkey doesn't bite me.'

'It's not far to go,' said Sue to Cocoa but he began to cry and kick and Mrs Smith put him down. 'You come home with us,' she told him. 'We'll have a big tea with chocolate biscuits and then we'll find Gan and Dan.'

This was very successful. Cocoa cheered up when they got him home, and as soon as he was well into a piece of pink iced cake, Sue dashed out to the back garden. 'I'll find his Gan,' she called and climbed up on the wall before her mother could say 'no'.

The washing was down now, so it was difficult to remember how far to go along the wall. She walked and walked, and looked for the lion cub, but she couldn't see it. Then she saw a pair of stilts, propped against the rear of a house. 'Is anyone there?' she called.

The lion cub came out of an old beer barrel, stretched slowly and looked at Sue, who wondered whether to go back and try to find the house from the street. But Cocoa wasn't scared of the lion cub, so why should she be afraid to go through the garden?

She jumped off the wall on to the pile of old newspapers and the lion cub growled, a small growl but definitely a growl. 'I'm a friend of Cocoa's,' she told it, rather feebly, in case it recognised the name. Then she walked as quickly as she dared without running to the back door, and knocked.

As she stood, she did not dare turn round in case the cub was creeping up behind her. If it pounced, it might knock her over, because it was quite fat, and its teeth looked very sharp.

The door was opened by a witch. She had a brown, wrinkled face, long black hair, gold earrings and . . . Sue jumped back several inches—a black

snake coiled round her skinny arm. At the same time, something furry brushed against Sue's legs. 'Oh!' she cried.

'It's only our Flossie. She won't hurt you,' said the witch. 'And Lance is all right.'

'Does Cocoa live here?' asked Sue.

The witch clutched Sue's shoulder with an iron hand. 'Do you know where he is?' she asked.

She looked at the snake's black head and at the little forked tongue that shot out so near her, and moved back a little while she explained about Cocoa. The lion cub gently gnawed her shoe and then licked her leg with a rasping tongue. She did hope he didn't like the taste so much that he took a bite.

'That Dan! I'll teach him to lose Cocoa. Dan!' called the witch, when Sue had finished explaining.

'Coming, Gran.' The boy who owned the stilts came to the door. 'Oh, it's you,' he said, frowning at Sue.

'She's found Cocoa,' said the witch.

Dan smiled broadly. 'Is he all right? And Christabel, the monkey?'

Sue nodded, and soon she and Dan were hurrying back along the wall to fetch Cocoa.

When they arrived at the garden, a familiar angry voice called out. 'Get down from my wall *at once*!'

Mrs Mudge was standing at the top of the steps that led down into the garden from the wooden balcony outside her sitting-room.

'Oh, dear,' said Sue and she slithered down from the wall.

'Why's the old girl so cross?' Dan asked in rather a loud voice.

'I've seen you before, you gypsy boy!' Mrs Mudge shouted. 'And I'll tell your mother, Susan, about the company you're keeping.'

'My mother knows I'm . . .' Sue began, then she remembered that her mother didn't know Dan was coming. 'Anyway, she won't mind,' she said defiantly.

'I can't have rowdy gypsy boys upsetting my tenants!' shouted Mrs Mudge, which was a silly remark, as both Miss Wilkinson and Mr Hyde were out at their work.

At that moment, Mrs Smith came to the basement back door. 'Is something wrong?' she asked.

'Climbing on my wall . . .' muttered Mrs Mudge.

'We found a lost child, and Susan has been collecting his brother,' said Mrs Smith.

(35)

'My house full of lost children!' snorted Mrs Mudge, but Sue's mother did not argue, and they followed her indoors.

'What a rude old woman!' Dan said, scowling fiercely. 'My dad would tell her where to get off.'

'She's our landlady, so we have to be nice to her or she might not let us stay,' Sue explained.

'All the same, I'd like to tell her what I think of her,' Dan said. 'Why don't you live in a caravan? Nobody bothers you there.'

'They cost a lot of money,' said Mrs Smith. 'And you can't live right in a town, either. It's difficult to get sites. Now, what shall we do about the little boy?'

Cocoa was fast asleep in an armchair with Christabel curled in his arms. It seemed a pity to wake them up, so Sue and Dan had tea and Dan told them all about himself. 'My father's a lion-tamer. He's called Daniel, like me, and he's terribly brave. We're staying near the town to see Gran and my aunt and uncle, and then we'll be going back to our winter quarters and do some work before we start touring.'

Cocoa woke up. 'Dan,' he said sleepily when he saw his brother, then he smiled happily.

'We'd better go home, Cocoa,' said Dan. 'How would you like to try my stilts tomorrow?' he asked Sue.

She saw that her mother looked doubtful. 'Could I, *please*?' she asked.

'Well, just round the garden here,' Mrs Smith agreed.

Sue was very happy, and so excited by the adventure that when Dan and Cocoa had gone she did a handstand against the wall and kept up while she counted five.

4

Dan, Cocoa and Christabel arrived next morning while Mrs Smith was still asleep. Sue saw them coming, through the window, and let them in quietly. Dan carried Cocoa's red tricycle through the kitchen-bathroom, into the garden, and the little boy walked it round and round while Dan helped Sue get on the stilts.

'Won't the monkey get giddy?' Sue asked, seeing what very small circles Cocoa made.

He shook his head. 'Christabel's trained for the circus. She rides on the back of a Shetland pony. She's named after my cousin, who's a bare-back rider.'

(37)

'Does she stand up on the horse?' Sue asked, as she took a tottering step forward.

'Of course. That's easy. Nothing to it,' he said.

Sue wished she could do it. At the moment, even walking on stilts seemed very difficult. After a few steps, she fell off.

Dan got on the stilts to show her. He could even do a little dance.

'Belle wants bikket,' said Cocoa.

'He means *he* wants a biscuit,' said Dan. 'He always pretends Christabel wants one.'

'I'll get some,' said Sue. Then she remembered something. 'Is he called Cocoa because he likes to drink it?' she asked.

'Silly! No, it's C O C O after the famous clown, because he's going to be a clown.'

When Sue came back with the biscuits she heard Mrs Mudge's loud and angry voice in the garden, crying, 'Take it off me!'

Christabel was sitting on Mrs Mudge's back holding on to her tightly curled, greasy hair.

'She thinks you're her mother!' Dan laughed so loudly that he nearly fell off his stilts.

'Take it off!' shouted Mrs Mudge.

Sue gently lifted Christabel off Mrs Mudge's

back and held the tiny monkey in her hands. Christabel wrapped her long tail round Sue's wrist and clutched at her fingers with doll-like hands. 'You see, she wouldn't hurt you,' Sue said to Mrs Mudge.

'No animals. That's what the rules are in this house. And I wish I'd said "no children", too,' said Mrs Mudge. Her face looked like a big red balloon, just about to pop. She must have seen them in the garden and hurried down the steps from her sitting-room. Sue's mother came to the kitchen door in her dressing-gown. When she heard what all the trouble was about, she tried to make Mrs Mudge see that Christabel was harmless, but it was no good. The monkey had to go, so Dan and Coco had to go, too.

'Cheer up,' Dan said quietly to Sue, who was almost crying. 'We'll leave Christabel at home next time.'

Sue cheered up, and when she walked with her mother past the garden in the square, she thought how much the other children playing there would like to know a lion-tamer's son, a future clown, and a lion cub and a monkey.

Dan and Coco came even earlier the following

morning, but Coco wouldn't follow Dan through the doorway. 'No. Want Belle,' he said, and his face grew red like Mrs Mudge's.

'She sleeps on his bed and goes everywhere with him,' explained Dan.

They tried to persuade Coco inside.

'I've got some toffees,' said Sue.

'I'll give you a pick-a-back,' said Dan.

But Coco's face grew more and more red and he shouted, 'No!'

'If I pick him up he'll scream,' said Dan.

At any moment Mrs Mudge might come along, and if Coco screamed she would probably stop them ever coming again.

'Can't you play in the street? It doesn't matter if he screams there,' said Dan.

'I'm not allowed to,' said Sue.

'I know! We'll go back to Gran's and you can go along the wall and meet us in her garden,' said Dan.

At that moment, Coco darted away from Dan, ran up the steps and got on his tricycle. He began to waddle very fast down the street.

'See you!' called Dan, and he went after Coco.

Sue went into the flat, thinking hard. If she

walked along the wall, her mother would be angry, but if she didn't meet Dan, he might never come and see her again. And she did so want to learn to walk on stilts. She would be so lonely without Dan.

She went into the garden, climbed up the wall and walked along as quickly as she could. Dan and Coco were already in the garden when she arrived, in a breathless heap, because she showed off and jumped.

'You'd never make an acrobat!' said Dan, and he laughed.

The lion cub got up from its bed of old newspapers and stared at Sue. She stared back and hoped she didn't look a bit nervous.

Coco, with Christabel clinging to his back, hugged the cub and immediately it lay down. Coco stroked its stomach, which it seemed to enjoy, stretching like a cat.

'Mind, Coco. You know what happens when old Lance gets playful,' said Dan. 'That's the trouble. He wouldn't hurt anyone but he doesn't know his own strength sometimes. Lance is named after my Uncle Lance who trains seals.'

Sue felt she would be safer on the stilts in case

Lance got playful, so she tried walking round the garden.

Suddenly the back door opened and the witch came out with the snake still coiled round her arm. Sue couldn't think of the witch as Gran and the snake still worried her. She was so busy looking at it that she didn't concentrate on her stilts, and fell over.

The next minute the witch was helping her up with the arm with the snake twisted round it.

'Oh!' said Sue.

'Don't be scared,' said Gran. 'Flossie's only a grass snake. Couldn't hurt you if she wanted to. Not like some I've known!' She cackled, just like a witch.

'Gran used to walk around *covered* in snakes,' said Dan. 'She did a snake-charming act.'

Sue shivered, but Gran persuaded her to stroke Flossie's head, and the skin was warm and dry, not slithery as she had expected.

As Gran went into the house, Dan said: 'I've an idea. You come and see my father. It's not far away. Then I'll show you the lions.'

'I'm not allowed in the streets,' Sue said sadly.

'We could walk along the wall. It goes the right

way. We don't need to cross any roads.'

'Mummy wakes up at half past eleven,' said Sue.

'It's only nine now,' said Dan. 'I heard the clock strike.'

So they set out, leaving Lance behind because Dan didn't think the cub would enjoy walking on the wall. Coco brought Christabel, of course, and Dan held the back of Coco's dungarees in case he slipped.

They had gone quite a long way, in the opposite direction to Sue's home, when someone shouted: 'Get off my wall!' and Sue saw a cross-looking woman waving a broom at them.

Coco started to run and would have fallen off the wall if Dan hadn't been holding on to him. Sue bumped into Dan, and nearly knocked him off the wall, and all the time the woman was shouting: 'Get off my wall!'

At last they left her behind and came to the end of the wall. Ahead was a playground. Sue had never been there before and she looked at the swings, the roundabout and the slides and wished she could play there every day.

It took a long time to go through the playground because Coco insisted (red-faced and stamping his foot) on trying everything, which Sue enjoyed, but she was anxious to see the lions and get home before her mother woke up.

At last Coco had been on the swings, the slide and the small children's roundabout, and Dan led them out of the playground and round the edge of a place where rubbish was dumped.

At last Dan said: 'There's the cottage,' and he pointed to a roof showing over a high stone wall.

A great roar greeted their arrival. 'That's Prince, showing off,' said Dan, and he opened a door in the wall. Coco rushed through and Sue followed them into a sort of yard, feeling very nervous. She did hope that Prince wasn't running loose inside.

No, there he was, in a cage near the cottage, with a lioness beside him. Again and again they roared, and Sue jumped each time. There was a caravan in the yard and a small man came out of it. He had black hair, like Dan's, and smiled in a friendly way. Sue was a little disappointed as she had imagined a lion-tamer would be large and fierce-looking, with a bristly moustache.

Dan said, 'Show her the lions, Dad. She found Coco when he was lost.'

Dan's father whistled, and out of the caravan

came a huge lioness. She gave a great roar and lashed her tail.

'Oh!' said Sue, as Coco rushed up to the lioness.

'Don't worry,' said Dan. 'Queenie, named after Gran, is very old. She's Lance's grandma. She's got hardly any teeth and she loves Coco.'

Queenie ran in a circle with Coco on her back. Then she gave Christabel a ride, and then she begged like a dog. Sue actually patted her, feeling very brave.

'Here's your elevenses,' said a comfortable-looking woman, coming out of the cottage. She carried a jug and cups on a tray.

'This is Dan's Aunt Rose,' said Dan's father. 'Sue's come to see the lions. She found Coco for us,' he said as Aunt Rose poured out the cocoa.

'Ah—he's a naughty little boy,' Aunt Rose said, smiling fondly at Coco. 'It's a good job you found him, Sue. Trouble is, since his mother died, all his aunts spoil him. And he's got eight of them! I'm the only one not in the circus. Used to be a bare-back rider but I gave up when I married Arthur. He drives one of those new diesels,' she added proudly. 'And this is Gran's old caravan.' She pointed to a gay, yellow caravan near the cottage.

'It's been spruced up, mind you, with a few modern bits and pieces. Gran gave it to me as a wedding present—that was before we got the cottage. Arthur finds a caravan too small. He's over six feet tall and almost as broad!' She laughed cheerfully and Sue liked her.

'Come on, Dad, get in the cage,' Dan said, when they had drunk their cocoa.

'All right—but it's not much of an act without all the props and the bigger cage,' said Dan's father, and he got into the cage. Sue shivered as Prince lashed his tail and Princess crouched down as if to spring. 'Lie down, my dears,' said Dan's father, and both lions lay down on their sides. He gently rubbed their tummies with his foot. 'That's about all I can do in this little cage,' he said to Sue, and came out.

'They looked very fierce at first,' Sue said.

'They're all right with me, treated properly,' said Dan's father. 'But you have to be careful. Sometimes they're a bit moody or irritable.'

Sue suddenly remembered that they had just had elevenses. 'What's the time?' she asked.

'Ten past eleven,' said Aunt Rose.

This was terrible! She'd never get back in time!

'Thank you very much for showing me everything. I must run all the way back,' she said, and she hurried off.

'Wait for us!' Dan called, but soon Coco's short legs were tired and Dan had to carry him, so she left them far behind as she went through the playground, up the wall, past the witch's house, and along the wall to home.

Mrs Smith was in her dressing-gown when Sue walked into the kitchen. 'Did you walk along the wall again?' she asked.

Sue tried to explain about Coco not wanting to come without Christabel. 'And so we went to see the lions and I patted one of them. Dan's father is so nice.'

'Well, I'm glad you've got some new friends,' said her mother. 'I like Dan and Coco but I think you'd better play with them here, and not go all that way again on your own. I'm afraid Mrs Mudge and the neighbours will complain if they see you walking on the wall.'

Sue felt a little sad. If Coco wouldn't come without Christabel, would Dan be able to come without Coco?

But Dan did come, alone, the following morning.

'Coco still wouldn't leave Christabel,' he said. 'And I've got to go back early because it's Gran's day for going out scrubbing and I'll have to keep an eye on Coco because Dad's busy.' He gave Sue the stilts, and sat down in the sunshine.

'We're joining the rest of the circus soon,' he went on. 'It's a pity you can't come and help with the animals.'

'Don't you go to school?' she asked.

'Of course. Wherever we are.'

Sue took four huge strides. Really, it was quite easy when you practised. 'I've got to go to my new school soon,' she said gloomily, thinking how lonely it would be when Dan had gone. Then, for a little while she forgot about school because she found she could walk all the way round the garden without falling off.

The time for Dan to go home came far too quickly, and Sue spent the rest of the day thinking about school and feeling sad.

5

Dan came again the next day. He came alone, carrying the stilts through the front door.

'Mummy was rather cross about my going to see

you,' said Sue. 'And she didn't really seem to believe that I'd patted a lion.'

'I've got something to ask her, when she wakes up,' Dan said mysteriously. 'If she says "yes" you'll be pleased.'

'Oh, what is it?' Sue asked.

'I won't say in case she says "no",' said Dan. 'Come on, let's try the stilts.'

Sue was just taking her fifth careful step, determined to go twice round the garden today, and Dan was calling out encouragingly, when '*Susan!*' shouted a familiar, angry voice. Sue fell off the stilts with a bump and looked up. Mrs Mudge was on her balcony, red-faced as usual, and her hair bristled with fierce-looking steel curlers. 'This will have to stop!' she went on. 'I saw you on the wall again the other day! Gypsy children all over my garden and on my wall . . .'

Dan looked at her, and his face was pale. 'You're a very rude old woman,' he said. 'We are not gypsies. We are artists, skilled performers, not keepers of lodging-houses, like you!' Sue had never heard him use such long words before. He stalked indoors, carrying the stilts and she followed him anxiously, hearing Mrs Mudge's gasp of fury.

'Oh, I do hope she doesn't turn us out,' she said.

Mrs Smith came out of the bedroom. 'Mrs Mudge?' she asked. 'I thought I heard voices.'

'She's been beastly to me again,' said Dan.

'She called him a gypsy, but I don't think *she* liked being called a keeper of a lodging-house,' said Sue.

'Well, we do have to be polite to her, Dan,' said Mrs Smith. 'But let's forget about it now. I'll have my tea and perhaps you'd like some lemonade, Dan, and biscuits?'

'What were you going to ask Mummy, Dan?' Sue asked.

Dan stopped frowning. 'Oh, yes. My father asked if Sue would like to travel with us to our winter quarters. It's only an hour's journey away.'

'Oh, please, Mummy,' Sue said excitedly.

'It's very kind,' said her mother. 'But how would Sue get back again?'

'I've thought of that,' Dan said. 'There's a coach that comes all the way back.'

'Well . . .' Sue's mother said doubtfully.

'Dad said you mightn't like the idea, so he wants you to have some food at the caravan tomorrow and then he says he'll talk you round.'

(52)

'Please, Mummy,' Sue said again.

'It's very nice of him . . .' Mrs Smith began.

'Noon tomorrow, then,' Dan said quickly. 'You'll not want to walk along the wall. The 93 bus takes you from here to Sandy Lane and we'll meet you there. Now, I've got to go home.'

'Oh, I'm longing to show you the lions, Mummy,' Sue said when Dan had gone.

'Does Dan's mother live at the caravan?' asked Mrs Smith.

'No. He hasn't a mother,' Sue said.

'Then I hope it's not going to be too much work for his father, cooking for us,' said Mrs Smith.

'Just think of eating in a real caravan!' said Sue.

All the way on the bus the next day, Sue wondered if Dan's father would be able to persuade her mother to let her go with them. 'There they are!' she said when they got off the bus. Coco was wearing a new red shirt and Christabel held a flag.

'I'm very pleased to meet you, Mrs Smith,' said Dan's father, and he really looked very pleased.

On the way to the caravan, Dan's father and Sue's mother talked away like old friends, and Sue and Dan smiled at each other. When they went into the yard, the lions roared a welcome and a wonderful smell of cooking wafted out of the caravan door.

Sue felt proud of her mother when they went inside and Queenie rose from the floor to greet them. Mrs Smith only hesitated a moment, then she put out her hand and Queenie came to lick it, with a huge, very pink tongue.

'Feels like sand-paper!' said Sue's mother.

'You've got courage, Mrs Smith,' said Dan's father. 'I've seen people turn and hurry out when they saw Queenie, even though I've told them she's toothless and as safe as houses.'

Mrs Smith smiled. 'You forgot to tell *me* she was toothless!' she said. 'But I love animals. We had a lovely cat before we came to the town. Cats are my favourites because they don't give their friendship easily, like dogs. You have to respect cats.'

'Yes, just like my lions,' Dan's father said approvingly. 'I always say it takes special people to get on with cats and lions. Those that want animals to make them feel big and bossy, they'll have a dog, but a cat, big or small, won't be pushed about. You've got to be partners.' Coco had been leaning on Queenie and now, as if to show she, too, had her pride, she pushed him away and went to sit in the corner, where Lance tried unsuccessfully to make her play with him.

(54)

The caravan was very tidy and clean, with a great deal of shining brasswork, and Mrs Smith exclaimed with pleasure at the neat little kitchen. 'A proper stove, too!' she said.

'Everything we need,' Dan's father said proudly. 'But you should see our own caravan. It's really modern. Now, food's ready!' He brought out a steaming dish and they had a most delicious meal of stew, dark and rich, followed by a chocolate pudding covered in cream. Lance came to sit by Dan, and watched him like a dog for titbits.

Coco had three helpings of everything and never said a word.

'Lovely,' said Mrs Smith.

'Mm,' said Sue.

'I like cooking,' said Dan's father. 'Now, how about this little jaunt for your Sue? I'd like to give her a treat after the way you found Coco for us. And I don't suppose it's much fun for her, having that landlady watching all the time. Nearly came round to give her a piece of my mind when I heard what she'd said to Dan here, but he said she might throw you out, so I didn't.'

'Yes, she's not very nice,' said Mrs Smith. 'I think she's cross because she's lonely and lonely because she's cross, if you know what I mean.'

'You're a kinder person than I am,' said Dan's father. 'Now, about this little trip tomorrow. She'd travel in the car with Dan and me, leaving bright and early. We'd put her on the bus to come back. Dan's found out it gets back just after tea, so you'd have plenty of time to meet her before you go out to work.'

Sue crossed her fingers, and looked at her mother.

'It's very kind of you,' said Mrs Smith. 'Sue should have a wonderful day.'

'Couldn't you come too?' asked Dan's father. 'Skip your rest for once?'

'I wish I could,' said Mrs Smith. 'But it isn't fair on the patients if I'm tired. I must get back now to have another sleep before I go on duty.' They followed her out of the caravan.

'I'm so glad I can come with you!' Sue said to Dan.

'Wait till you see the elephants!' he said happily.

Aunt Rose bustled out of the cottage. 'Just got back,' she said. 'I work mornings in a sweet-shop. Did he give you a good meal? I wanted to leave something to heat up, but no, he's always independent. A good cook, for a man, I will say!' She smiled at Mrs Smith.

'This is Sue's mother,' said Dan's father. 'Aunt Rose is the only one of us not in the circus.'

'Come and have a cup of tea with me,' Aunt Rose said.

'I wish I could,' said Mrs Smith. 'But I've a job to do, myself.'

'Could I go back along the wall?' Sue asked her mother.

'Better not, after all the fuss Mrs Mudge has been making lately,' said her mother.

'That's not a good place for you to live,' said Dan's father.

'Just have to make the best of it,' said Mrs Smith. She and Sue thanked him. 'I've not enjoyed anything so much for a long time,' and Mrs Smith smiled, looking really happy, instead of pretending, as she usually did.

On the way back, she said, 'What friendly people they are! I liked them as soon as I saw them.'

Sue was so excited that she woke up very early the following day. She put her light on and saw it was six o'clock. She put on her blue jeans (which she had last worn at their cottage) in case there was any elephant riding, and then tiptoed into the kitchen to get her breakfast. She was too excited to be very hungry, and it didn't take long to eat her cornflakes and wash the plate. Then she went to sit by the window and watch for Dan. First she saw the milkman's feet and heard the clink of bottles on the step, then she saw some unfamiliar, early-morning feet, and the little piece of pavement was lit by sunshine, so it was going to be a fine day. She wondered why time always went so slowly when you were waiting, and galloped along when you were doing something nice, and then at last she saw an old pair of sand-shoes, followed by a very small pair of red shoes, and felt sure it was Dan and Coco.

She hurried out of the door into the hall. Instantly, Mrs Mudge's kitchen door opened. 'Where are *you* off to?' asked Mrs Mudge. Her greasy hair was tightly wound into her enormous metal curlers and Sue wondered if she had been sleeping in the kitchen all night.

There was a knock at the outside door, and Mrs Mudge flew to open it before Sue could. 'Go away!' she shouted. 'Disturbing my house at this hour!' Sue tried to get past her enormous bulk.

'Coming,' Sue called to Dan and Coco.

'This is a respectable square and no place for boys like you with dirty monkeys . . . Oh!' Mrs Mudge shouted, as Christabel leaped on to her head and at the same time Coco furiously butted her legs.

'Stop it!' said Dan and Sue, but it was too late. Mrs Mudge collapsed to the floor. Christabel chattered with surprise and jumped on to Mrs Mudge's stomach.

Mrs Smith opened the door of their flat. 'Whatever has happened?' she asked, looking at the strange sight in the hall.

Dan seized Coco because he looked as if he were going to follow Christabel on to Mrs Mudge's stomach, and the monkey leaped to his shoulder.

'Help me!' panted Mrs Mudge.

Sue and Mrs Smith pulled her up with difficulty, for she was as heavy as a sack of coal.

'I'm giving you a week's notice, Mrs Smith,' puffed Mrs Mudge. 'Disturbed at all hours . . .' There was a fierce roar from the street.

'That's Prince and Princess and Queenie,' said Dan. 'Dad's got the trailer there.'

'Wild animals everywhere!' exclaimed Mrs Mudge. 'And attacks by gypsy boys!'

'You were rude to them,' Sue told her bravely.

'Say sorry you bumped her,' Dan told Coco, whose face was as red as Mrs Mudge's.

'Not sorry. Hate her!' said Coco.

'I'm sorry he bumped you,' Dan said, but Sue could see he was only trying to help; he wasn't sorry at all.

'You'd better go or you'll be late, Sue,' said her mother.

'But we've nowhere to live,' Sue said, almost crying.

'Don't worry, we'll be all right,' said her mother. 'Have a nice day.'

'And you let her go with those awful boys . . .' Sue heard Mrs Mudge say as they went up the steps.

'Oh *dear*,' said Sue.

'You'd be better off if you did leave,' said Dan.

'Not if we haven't anywhere to live,' Sue said gloomily. 'But Mummy's very good at making people un-cross, so perhaps she'll make Mrs Mudge change her mind.'

'She told you not to worry,' said Dan. 'You'd better forget all about it today.'

'You've been long enough,' Dan's father said as

they got into the car that pulled the trailer.

They told him what had happened.

'Dear me. The nasty old thing!' he said. 'I'm very sorry Coco upset her.'

'He did, too, right over!' Dan laughed, and they all joined in and felt much better.

6

Soon they were driving through open country.

The sun shone, and everywhere was bright green with new leaves and tender young grass. Sue forgot all about Mrs Mudge, especially when she saw some tiny lambs and their mothers.

Lance sat on the back seat with Coco, Christabel and Dan, packed closely together, so Sue offered to change places.

'No. Coco's asleep,' whispered Dan. 'I don't want to wake him or he'll get all wriggly.'

Sue looked round, and saw Coco cuddled up to Lance, both of them fast asleep, with Christabel curled up on Lance's back.

The road went up a very steep hill, through a beech wood and then Dan shouted, 'Look!' Far below, in a grassy valley, was a small farmhouse, and a cluster of tents, caravans and sheds. Ponies of all colours grazed in a field nearby.

'Could I ride a pony?' Sue called excitedly, as they drove down the hill.

'She could try old Sugar, couldn't she, Dad?' Dan suggested.

'If your cousin Christabel isn't busy practising a new act,' he answered.

They drove into the field beside the farm, and parked alongside one of the caravans. Two men, who had been mending a tent, stopped work and came up, and a girl with long fair hair, busy feeding a yapping mass of dogs, waved and smiled.

'Hullo! Back to do a bit of work at last,' said one of the men.

'These are more of the family, Sue,' Dan's father said. 'My brother Alex and his son, Lance. Sue found Coco when he was lost,' he explained. 'We thought she'd like a day here. Doing any rehearsing today, Lance?'

'My seals could do with a run-through,' Lance said. He looked rather like a seal himself with big dark eyes and sleek black hair. 'I'm teaching them a new act.'

'I'll be glad to leave the tent for a bit, too,' said

Lance's father. 'My youngsters need a bit of practice for next week.'

'This way,' said Dan's father, and they followed him to the big barn beside the farmhouse. Inside, under the glare of a floodlight, lots of things seemed to be happening at once. There was a proper ring in the centre, with thick peat, and a piebald pony cantered round slowly with a girl standing on its back. 'Hullo, Christabel,' called Dan. 'This'll be her first season, Sue. She's just fifteen,' he said. 'That's her mother, my Aunt Miranda,' and he pointed to the far side of the ring, where Aunt Miranda was walking along a wire fixed between two supports, with a tray full of glasses on her head.

Above them, two men swung backwards and forwards on two trapezes hanging from the roof. Sue was glad to see a safety net below them.

'Do you practise hard all the winter?' Sue asked.

'Not all the acts,' said Dan's father. 'But any new routines and of course the young animals who are being trained.'

'And *they* practise all the year round, like the acrobats,' said Dan, pointing upwards, where now one man jumped and was caught by the other. 'Those are my second cousins, Matthew and

Martin, the twins. They're so good they went to London to a big Christmas circus.'

'Don't you do anything at Christmas, then?' asked Sue.

'Oh yes,' said Dan's father. 'Near here we hire a hall and give shows, and we do a miniature indoor circus for big parties at factories and so on.'

'But there's a lot of dull work as well,' said Dan. 'Mending the tent, painting the vans . . .'

'See who's talking! You always say you've got too much homework to help,' said his father.

'What about the holidays?' Dan asked. 'I'm very overworked then.'

His father laughed.

'Could we give Sue a bit of a show?' Dan asked. 'I'll be Ringmaster, as Uncle Edward's away.'

'See what the others think,' his father said. 'Alex and Lance will be along soon. You get your lot.'

Sue wondered what Dan's 'lot' was, as he and Coco rushed off, followed by Lance who was now at the end of a long lead.

'Have a ride?' Christabel asked Sue. 'Sugar's as safe as a rocking-horse.'

Sue got on the pony from the side of the ring. Sugar's back felt very wide and slippery and Sue

clung to the pommel in front of her as the pony walked round.

'Try going faster,' Christabel suggested.

'All right,' Sue said rather nervously.

'Canter, Sugar,' said Christabel, and the pony immediately broke into a slow, easy stride. Sue had only once before ridden a pony, at a fair, but she was determined not to look frightened so she clung hard to the pommel, flopping up and down as Sugar cantered.

'Good for you!' called Christabel. 'Walk, now, Sugar,' she ordered, and the pony slowed down, just as Sue wondered how she could possibly manage to stay on another minute, and she slid off thankfully.

Suddenly, Dan trotted into the ring, riding a small black pony, followed by Coco on a smaller black pony, followed by Christabel the monkey holding the stubby mane of a tiny black foal. They cantered round once, and then Dan and Coco made their ponies kneel to Sue, while Christabel held the foal's halter.

'Our first act,' Dan said. 'Starting next week, when we have our first one day stand. I had to talk like mad to get Dad to agree and then it'll only be on Saturdays, because we can't miss school. Of course, I can do proper tricks on a horse.' He vaulted on to Sugar's back and made her canter round the ring, standing on her back as Christabel had done. 'Watch me!' he shouted, and stood on one leg. Sue clapped, but as she did, Dan fell off and sprawled in the peat.

'Serves you right for showing off,' said his father, and Coco laughed delightedly as poor Dan got up, looking cross.

There was a great barking and yapping and twelve dogs streamed into the barn, followed by the girl Sue had just seen.

'My cousin Lara and her famous troop of performing dogs,' Dan called out in a ringmaster-ish voice.

'I'll just run them through their act for you,' said Cousin Lara and she sent her dogs over little fences that Dan's father put in the ring; they waltzed on their hind legs, jumped over each other, through a hoop, and one little white poodle jumped on to Sugar's back and balanced while she cantered round the ring. After their tricks, they all had bits of biscuit as a reward.

Sue clapped hard, and then Dan said, 'Look!'

She turned and saw the huge bulk of an elephant. Its back just skimmed the top of the barn door and its trunk weaved affectionately towards the tall man who walked in front.

'Lulu, Lisa and Lilly,' announced Dan, as two more elephants followed the first, each holding on to the tail in front. 'Trained by Uncle George.'

Dan and Christabel took the ponies out of the ring, and Uncle George led the elephants in. 'Like a ride?' he asked Sue.

'Oh, yes, please,' she answered.

He made Lulu kneel and helped Sue on to her back. 'Hold tight to her collar,' he said, and Lulu got up. Sue felt a very long way from the ground and it was strange to sit on the elephant's neck, behind the great, flapping ears, but Lulu walked slowly round the ring and Sue pretended she really was in the circus, dressed in spangles and tights, with people clapping and the band playing. When Lulu knelt down again, it was like a grey mountain collapsing, and Sue held on very hard, before sliding to the ground.

Uncle George got the elephants to stand on their hind legs with their front legs on the back of the elephant in front, and Sue clapped.

'Let her see your act with Lulu,' Dan said eagerly and Uncle George lay down right underneath the elephant while she bent her legs until she almost touched him and Sue held her breath. Lulu got up again, stepped carefully over Uncle George and Christabel gave her a large currant bun.

Suddenly the waiting ponies scattered in alarm.

'Lance!' called Dan.

A yellow streak darted in and out of the ponies' legs and rushed out of the barn.

'I told you always to hold his lead,' Dan's father said.

'He pulled it right out of my hand,' Dan said.

Before they had time to go after him, Dan's Uncle Alex came into the barn, holding Lance's lead in one hand and grasping a chimpanzee's hand in the other, while two more chimps followed him.

'Caught your runaway!' he said.

'You'll have to train him a bit better, Dan,' said his father.

The chimps looked happier when Lance was back with Dan, and they gave Sue a little show. One of them rode a small bicycle round the ring, another rode the piebald pony, waving an arm as she cantered along, and the other played a drum and did a little dance. Like all the other animals, they had a little titbit to reward them.

'I'm also Zozo, the Clown,' said Uncle Alex, and he did lots of somersaults, handstands and cart-wheels very quickly, then pranced round the ring on stilts, making jokes and sometimes falling off. Dan's father went into the ring. 'I do an act with Zozo,' he said. 'But it's not the same without the clothes, and the water squirters and the flour and custard pies to throw!'

Sue laughed, all the same, and the chimps sat in a row and clapped their hands.

'My aunts are busy mending costumes and making new ones,' Dan said. 'I wish you could see the bright colours and hear the music. We have to be ready to start touring next week.'

'Aren't you lucky!' Sue sighed. 'It must be fun.'

'Hard work,' Dan's father said. 'Up at six every morning and off on the road. Then a good old rush to get the tent up, animals fed and everything fixed up for the show. And then, unless we're to stay two days, down it all has to come and everything stowed away. We're not in bed till midnight. You can imagine how much we welcome the places where we stay two days.'

'I didn't know it was like that,' Sue said, and she stopped feeling quite so envious of Dan.

'Uncle Lance and his amazing seals, Stanley, Sylvester and Slinky,' Dan announced, as the seals came in, flip-flop, looking rather out of place in a barn.

'Belle wants bikket,' Coco said.

'If Coco's hungry it must be time to eat,' said Dan's father.

'Yes, Nancy said you were to hurry up before the food's spoilt,' said Uncle Lance. 'So I'll just show you one or two quick tricks.'

The seals were very clever, balancing balls on their noses, and then flip-flopping up a plank without dropping the balls, and even playing a kind of catch.

Sue clapped hard at the end and then Coco said, 'Come *on*', and they all went to a big blue-and-red caravan, where Aunt Nancy, wearing a nylon over-all over a neat dress (Sue had half expected her to wear gypsy clothes), gave them large helpings of roast chicken, sausages, roast potatoes and peas, followed by a very satisfactory treacle tart.

Aunt Nancy was friendly and asked Sue all sorts of questions about home. 'It does seem a shame

that you've got such a nasty landlady,' she said
thoughtfully.

'Come on, let's see the ponies,' Dan said, after
they had eaten the last crumb and Coco had been
carried, drooping, to his rest.

They went to the field and Dan and Coco's little
black shetland ponies came up for sugar, followed
by the piebald and four small golden ponies. 'Oh,
aren't they sweet!' Sue said.

'You should see them, pulling their little coach
with Christabel inside, dressed as a fairy queen,'
Dan said. 'They pull Cinderella's coach at Christmas, too, in pantomimes. I do wish you could see
a real show of ours. Come to think of it, you could!
We're doing a show in May in the field next to
Uncle Arthur's cottage. You come along, Sue. You
and your mother must have free tickets, of course.'

'Thank you very much,' said Sue, and she
stopped feeling gloomy about saying goodbye at
the end of the day and picked a big bunch of
primroses for her mother. Then she walked on
Dan's stilts, and Aunt Nancy came out of her
caravan and told Sue she was getting very good
at it.

'I've something else to show you,' Dan said. He

led her to a shed. In the corner was a black poodle with six puppies, like fluffy black sausages, asleep at her side.

'Oh!' said Sue, and when she knelt down, one of the puppies woke up, lifted its tiny head, which had a white splodge on it, and gave a small yap.

'Pick him up,' Dan suggested. 'It's all right, Dinah,' he said to the mother, patting her.

The puppy was very warm and soft in her hands and he had a white patch on his chest to match his nose. He chewed at Sue's finger with miniature, needle-sharp teeth.

'He's lovely,' Sue said, stroking him gently.

'I know what!' Dan said excitedly. 'You have him! We're going to sell the others, because we've got enough dogs, but we'd not get much for him because of those white patches.'

'Could I really have him?' Sue asked excitedly. Then she remembered Mrs Mudge. 'Oh, no, we can't have a puppy in our flat.'

'Bother that unfriendly old landlady!' growled Dan.

'Dan!' called his father. Sue very sadly put the puppy back and followed Dan. His father was feeding Prince and Princess in their cage, while

Queenie ate something out of a bowl on the grass outside. Lance was next to her, copying his parents as they tore at their meat and growled.

'Poor old Queenie has to have the slops,' Dan said. 'A pity lions can't have false teeth!'

'I'm afraid it's nearly time for your bus, Sue,' said Dan's father.

She was sad again. 'I don't want to go,' she said.

'Cheer up. I've something to tell you,' Dan's father said. 'Nancy had an idea, and we've made a telephone call from the farmhouse. Uncle Arthur and Aunt Rose are pleased too, and so is your mother, because your landlady is still giving you a week's notice.'

'Oh, dear!' said Sue. 'So what is everyone pleased about?'

'I've been feeling we're a bit to blame for your having to move,' said Dan's father. Sue did wish that grown-ups weren't so slow in telling you things. 'So I thought of that caravan of Rose's. They let it in the summer, usually, but keep it for us in the winter. Well, that's a waste, isn't it? Next winter we'll bring our own caravan up when we go to see Gran. Lance can drive the lions up for me— I have to feed them myself, always, you see, and a change would upset them . . .'

'But I don't see . . .' Sue began.

'Oh—I thought I'd told you,' he said. 'Your mother's going to rent the caravan all the year. It'll help Arthur and it'll help her.'

'Live in a caravan! Oh, how lovely!' said Sue.

'Your mother was worried about the nights, but Rose will keep an eye on you.'

'She needs a dog for company,' Dan said quickly. 'That puppy of Dinah's with the white patches— Lara was grumbling about him . . .'

'What a good idea!' said his father. 'You have him, Sue, with love from us all. I'll drop him in to you when we start touring next week. He'll be just the right size for a caravan.'

Sue was hardly able to believe it was all really happening, and then she got into the car with Dan, Lance and Dan's father. Coco came running out of the caravan with Christabel on his shoulder. 'Don't go! Don't go!' he shouted. Dan's father tooted, and suddenly everyone came hurrying out of the barn and the caravans.

'Goodbye, Sue!' they called, and the uncles and aunts and cousins waved and called, while from a distant barn came the very strange trumpeting of an elephant.

'Goodbye!' called Sue.

'See you again!' called Aunt Nancy, and then the car moved off.

They drove to the bus stop and Sue only just had time to thank Dan's father before the bus came.

'We'll see you in the summer!' Dan called and Sue waved and waved until the bus went round the corner. She sighed. It was a long time until next summer and she would miss Dan so much. Then she remembered the puppy and knew she would never be lonely again. 'I shall call it Coco the Second,' she whispered. 'Then I'll think of the circus all the time. It looks a bit like a clown, with those white splodges.'

When she got out of the bus and saw her mother waiting for her, Sue was suddenly worried about Coco the Second. Would her mother mind?

'Did you have a lovely day?' Mrs Smith asked as Sue got off. 'And how is the latest member of the family?'

'How did you know?' Sue asked in surprise. 'Do you mind?' she added anxiously.

'I like puppies as much as you do,' said Mrs Smith. 'And he'll be good company for you when I'm out. Dan's father telephoned me again, while you were on the bus, to persuade me to have the puppy. But I thought it a good idea right away, even if I do like cats best. And isn't it lovely about the caravan? The rent is quite low and I'll only have fifteen minutes on the bus to the hospital.'

'It's all wonderful!' Sue said.

'Wonderful,' she said again, to Coco the Second, a week later, when she was tucked up in bed with the puppy curled at her feet. Their new home looked so cosy and friendly and tonight no Mrs Mudge would bend over her, smelling of moth-balls and onions.

'Not asleep yet?' Aunt Rose asked, looking into the tiny bedroom. 'I've a message from Dan's father. He wondered if you'd like an old pair of stilts he's left with us. Then you can practise and surprise Dan when the circus comes.'

'Thank you, I'd like to do that,' Sue said, and when Aunt Rose had gone back to her cottage, Sue snuggled down and thought how happy she was. Now they had a proper home, a dog, new friends and her very own stilts, and none of it would have happened if she had not seen Dan on his stilts out of the window and wanted to solve the mystery of the wooden legs.

Sue smiled to herself, said, 'Goodnight, Coco,' and went to sleep.

Seven White Pebbles

HELEN CLARE

Illustrated by Cynthia Abbott

I

Saturday

This story is about the youngest. There are often stories about the eldest, and the way she leads the others. But Polly Flower was the youngest of her family, and she was just eight. There are good things about being the youngest. Sometimes you are let off doing things which the others have to do. And if your sisters are feeling friendly they look after you. But if they are feeling nasty they may easily tease you. Also, you may be told you are not old enough to do this, that and the next thing. Or you have to go to bed when the others can stay up. These are the bad things about being the youngest: so perhaps it is even in the end.

Polly had two sisters. Jane was tall for twelve, and she had dark red hair and dark blue eyes. She talked a lot, and what she said made the others laugh. She did things quickly before she had time to think. She was very strong and brave, and Polly thought she was wonderful.

Melissa was nearly ten, and Polly thought she was the prettiest girl at school. Her hair was almost black and her eyes were large and grey. She did not talk so much as Jane. But when the three of them were together they often talked all at once and nobody could hear anything at all.

Polly had brown, ordinary hair and her face was not as pretty as Melissa's and her legs had not so nice a bulge below the knee. She could not play the piano at all, while Jane could play it really well already. She was not neat with her hands and good at games as Melissa was. When Polly said sadly to her mother that she wished she could do this, that and the other like Jane and Melissa, her mother told her that she was light on her feet, that she could sing in tune, as they all could, and that she was good at lessons.

'Anyway,' said Mrs Flower, 'everybody is herself, a person who has never happened before, in the whole wide history of the world. Think of that.'

Polly thought of it, and it seemed very strange and important.

'Never before? Never anybody like me?'

'Maybe somebody like you, but never, never Polly Flower before.'

'And ever again?'

'Never again. You're you, you know it.'

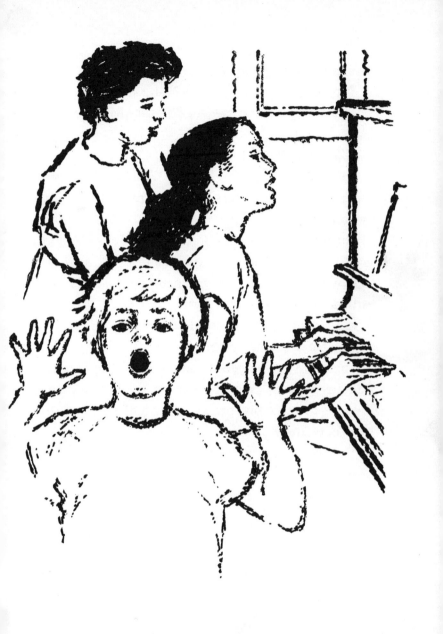

This seemed solemn. Perhaps it led to the strange thing Polly thought of next.

'Where is yesterday, today?' she said.

'I know no more than you do,' said Mrs Flower. 'Isn't it strange?'

'Who does know? God?'

'Probably,' said Mrs Flower. And she thought to herself that the things Polly said made her Polly, and not Melissa or Jane.

The story begins on a Saturday, which is a good day to begin as there is no school. There was no homework even for Jane, because it was the last Saturday of the summer term.

So Jane and Melissa and Polly were at the piano singing their holiday chant. It was a made-up tune of Jane's and she played the chords loudly and with prancing fingers as if she were a famous person. She sang in a wobbly, grown-up voice, which made the others laugh.

'This time next week where shall we be?' sang Jane.

'At the sea, at the sea!' sang the others.

'This time next week what shall we wear?'

'We hope we shall be almost bare.'

'This time next week what shall we eat?'

'Shrimps that we have caught in our net!'

This was not exactly a rhyme, but their mother said it was quite all right, it was a half-rhyme. There were many verses and the Flowers were always making up new ones.

Jane shut the piano.

'Come on,' she said.

'Mummy,' said Jane, running into the kitchen, 'as you're so busy, shall we all get out of your way by going up to the Hurst and having a good morning mucking around?'

'Yes,' said Mrs Flower. 'Be back at a quarter to one. Look after Polly.'

'I don't need looking after,' said Polly.

'Come on, we'll take the rope and be rock-climbers,' said Jane.

So they ran out of the house all talking at once, and down their road to the main road. Jane took hold of Polly by the collar and however much Polly tugged, Jane would not let go until they were safely over.

The Hurst was a wooded hill for ever, and nobody could build houses on it. Just as Polly Flower was herself for ever. And where yesterday was she could not think. She was breathless with

keeping up with the others. On top of the Hurst was an open grassy space, with some glorious trees to climb. On the other side was a fearsome slope, which Jane always made them rock-climb.

This slope was steep, and it was covered with grey and white pebbles. As you struggled up, these all rolled under your feet, and it was quite as bad as roller-skates, if not worse. Polly's legs were shorter than her sisters'.

'Come on, Polly, you're like a great piece of meat in the butcher's,' said Melly.

'Let's untie Polly and she can mountaineer alone,' said Jane. 'Shall we, Pie?'

They often called her Pie.

'I needn't do it at all,' said Polly. 'I can do something else I've thought of.'

Polly often made games of her own, when she wanted a rest from keeping up with the others. She pottered along the side of the Hurst looking for special pebbles. She chose seven, as white and smooth as she could find, and put them in her pocket. Below her a little way off she saw another girl who seemed busy. Polly looked down to see what she was doing and suddenly lost her balance. She started to run. If you once do this on a steep slope it is hard to stop yourself. Polly could not. She ran on down until a small, flat ledge half-stopped her and she rolled over.

'You beast! You clumsy, stupid, hateful beast!' screamed the girl, and she ran at Polly before she could get up and pushed her hard with both hands. Polly rolled the rest of the way to the bottom, it was not far to go now. She was very surprised, and very sore. Her hands and knees were scratched and she had a bruised eye where she had hit a stone.

'I say, what are you doing to my sister?' came Jane's voice from the top of the slope.

Jane's voice was very loud and brave and ready

to be angry. Polly could hear her, and felt glad.

'She's a beast! She's ruined my grotto! She's stamped all over it, the clumsy elephant—' The girl was crying now.

'She couldn't have done it on purpose. What grotto? Where?' said Melly, coming to see.

The girl had built a lovely grotto. She had found a small flat platform on the slope. A seedling tree grew on one side of it, only a few inches high. She had scooped out the earth from the slope behind the platform, and made a cave. The floor of the cave was laid with pebbles in a pattern. There was a path over the platform which led to it. At one side of the ledge she had built a tiny wall. There was a garden in front with patches of different moss, the velvet kind, and the kind with little green or yellow flowers. Twigs were stuck into the garden, too. Polly's foot had squashed the garden, but you could still see the remains.

'Oh, isn't it lovely,' Melissa said.

'It was,' said the girl angrily.

'Pie, look what you've done,' said Jane.

Polly scrambled up to look. She felt hurt in her body and her feelings. She peered into the cave and saw the remains of the garden.

'But I didn't mean to,' she said. 'I'm sorry.'

'You ran straight on to it,' scowled the girl.

'She's said she's sorry and you ought to take it,' ordered Jane. 'Shall we help you mend the garden? The cave's all right.'

Melissa found more twigs and moss and pebbles, and the garden soon looked even better than before.

Polly sat miserably watching. She felt rather sick, and her eye began to hurt.

'Poor old Pie,' said Jane, 'it wasn't your fault. Come on, it's time we went home. You can hold on to me and be a wounded soldier.'

Polly felt better at once. She hung on to Jane's

waist and down they went from the Hurst and home. Melissa came skipping along with the rope.

At bed-time Polly laid her pebbles on the window sill, one for each day, until they went to the sea. Then she pushed off Saturday and down it went, plop, on to the path.

'Look at my pebbles, Mummy. I was getting them when I spoilt that girl's grotto. I've pushed off today. But we still don't know where it really goes, do we?'

'No, we don't,' said Mrs Flower, kissing her.

'Oh, mind my bruise!' said Polly. And her mother did.

Polly lay listening to Jane practising the piano. She thought how clever and brave Jane was, and how well she had arranged things with the girl. She loved Jane's tinkly pieces. There was Grieg. And there was Schubert, who reminded her of sherbet. There was Beethoven (which you did NOT say like 'beetroot'). And there was Bach. If you called it Bark (like a dog) Jane said you were ignorant and a baby. You had to do a kind of choke at the end. Polly practised it.

'What are you doing, Polly?' called Mrs Flower.

'Saying Bach,' said Polly.

'Saying what? Oh, Bach. I thought you were being sick. Good-night, precious.'

'Good-night,' Polly said, laughing to herself.

2

Sunday

Polly loved the Sundays that they went to Grandma's. Grandpa used to drive up from Sussex where they lived, in his old motor-car, and meet the whole family after church. Grandma always had a lovely lunch for them, hot and ready. Grandpa was coming today.

Because of this, everyone was busy getting ready to be out for the whole day. Polly had combed her hair and was at the bottom of the garden. She had forgotten all about being stiff. Only her eyebrow hurt a little if she pressed it.

In her pocket she had one or two extra pebbles. She was tossing them in the air, trying to catch them both at once. If only she could juggle, to show Melissa and Jane! If only she could even throw well at cricket! Jane had said yesterday in the garden that Polly had no throw at all, but that she might suddenly get it, like whistling. And then she had

said that she betted she could throw a ball in at her window, and Melly had said she had better jolly well not.

Polly looked up at her own window. One side was half open, as her mother had told her to leave it. The pebble felt round and smooth and light in her hand. She was quite sure she could throw it in at the window, as Jane said. She felt she had suddenly got her throw. You did it over-arm, and you swung your arm so that it acted like a sling for the stone. Polly bent her whole body back, swung her arm as Jane said, and aimed at the open window. It felt lovely when the pebble flew.

There was a fearful, distant tinkle. Oh! The pebble did not come back. It must have gone in somewhere. Oh! Could she really have broken the window? Polly went hot all over. She pretended she had not done it. She turned her back and tossed the other pebble quickly up and down. She dared not look at her window at all. Had anybody heard, or seen? Surely Jane or Melly would hear and rush and tell their mother?

But no. Nothing happened at all. In a few minutes, they all came out, and her father called from the front garden:

'Ready, Poll?'

And Polly ran round and they all went to church. Polly sang very loudly and with her whole heart, hoping to feel good, but it was no use. She simply felt sick in her inside when she thought of the window and the tinkle. It was like a great, grey cloud over the day.

And there was Grandpa, waiting for them outside. Even the smell of Grandpa's tweed jacket was not quite so nice as usual when she hugged him. If only the others were not so near, Polly thought, as they drove off, and she cuddled up to her mother, she would tell her now. Whisper it. But somehow she could not do it. It was no good.

Grandma had an even better lunch than usual. It was roast chicken, and raspberries and cream.

'I'm letting the children pick the raspberries,' she said. 'Go on, dears, you've got twenty minutes. It will be the last lot.'

'Oh good,' Jane said. 'Come on.'

They loved picking the raspberries. They took a square punnet each and ran down Grandpa's long, windy, exciting garden. It was long and narrow, and full of delightful things. Everybody loved it. Grandpa's raspberries were huge, and juicy, and never had maggots on them. Polly picked and picked.

'Are you eating any?' said Jane to the others.

'No,' said Melly, 'we'd better not.'

'I've eaten one,' said Polly quickly.

'Let's all eat one. Only one,' ordered Jane.

Melly and Jane chose the biggest they could see and ate it. Polly thought how lovely it was down here, and then she thought of the window. Oh dear. Should she tell Jane and Melly?

'What's the matter with Polly? She seems very quiet,' she heard Grandma say later.

'The poor child fell head over heels down that rather steep slope from the Hurst yesterday,' said her mother.

'Poor wee soul,' said Grandma, and she was extra kind to Polly and gave her a special striped Grandma-peppermint to suck, like a snail shell. This was awful. Polly did not know how to say that she did not deserve it.

In Grandma's garden, near the end, was a huge grove of hollyhocks, and being in them was like being in a forest of flowers: yellow and cream and pink and apricot and red and almost black. Bees, powdery with pollen, bumbled from one to the next. Polly thought that a flower turned downwards would make a lovely skirt for a small doll. As for the little round boxes of seeds, they were like purses of dolls' pennies. Polly was happy in the hollyhock forest, until she thought of the window.

There was also a bed of rhubarb with huge, simply huge leaves. In the summer Grandpa would always say that the rhubarb had 'gone too far'. Polly could not understand this when she was little, because the rhubarb was there and had not gone anywhere at all. But she now knew that he meant it had grown too big to be eaten. But it was perfect

for crawling under. Or you were allowed to take a garden knife from the dark potting-shed, and cut a huge leaf for a sunshade. Polly did this, and so did Melissa, and their faces looked green and mysterious as they sat underneath them.

It was late when they started for home. The motor-car was full, as Grandma came too, so Polly lay along the people's knees at the back. Her head was in her mother's arm, and her feet were in Grandma's lap, and Melissa was in the middle. Jane was between her father and grandfather in front. It was such a warm, starry, scented night, Grandpa put the hood back. Polly gazed up at the dark blue sky and the stars which seemed to sing. She wondered why she was not all of her happy. Then she thought of the window.

'Mummy, look at that bird!' Melissa said. 'Swishing about!'

'It's a bat, darling. They fly at night.'

'I've never seen one before,' Polly said.

'Honeysuckle!' said Jane, sniffing. Jane smelt scents before anyone.

But at last they were home, and at last Polly dragged her feet up the stairs and turned the handle of her door, and went in. And Mrs Flower came behind to help her, as it was late. Before she turned on the light, they both saw.

The moon shone through a round hole in the window, and silver streaks spread out from it, like a silver spider's web.

'Polly, your window!' said her mother.

Polly said nothing.

'What happened?' said Mrs Flower.

'It was one of my pebbles,' said Polly softly. 'I was on the lawn.'

'But you know the rule,' said her mother.

Polly did. Never throw balls towards the house and never throw stones at all.

'What's she done?' said Jane, bouncing in.

'Gosh!' said Melly. 'Did you throw something, Polly?'

'Go away,' said Polly, but she felt half-pleased all the same. It proved she could throw.

Crunch, crunch went Mrs Flower's feet on the bits of glass.

'Come on, Pie, skin a rabbit,' she said, taking off Polly's dress. 'No pocket money, I'm afraid, for quite a time.'

'Mummy! It's the holiday! And Mummy, it's Melly's birthday! Please, Mummy, need I miss it till after Melly's birthday?'

'You'll have to make her something.'

'But she won't like it!'

'Yes, she will. We'll think of something.'

Polly's tears did not fall until she cleaned her teeth, and then they jerked out and got mixed with the toothpaste froth.

'Now knock off your pebble, chicken,' her mother said.

Polly knocked off Sunday. Clomp, it fell, on to the path, sounding gloomy.

'I should think you're glad to see it go, aren't you? You silly juggins. What a horrible day you must have had.'

'Oh, I *did*,' said Polly, hugging her mother hard.

3

Monday

On Monday Polly was home from school before the others. So she had tea with her mother, just the two of them, and then she fetched her doll Blackberry and went off into the garden to the swing which hung from the cherry tree branch.

She held her doll between her knees. She swung and looked up into the cherry tree. Several large blackbirds and starlings went flapping away, squawking. Polly could see a few fat cherries here and there, but she could also see a lot of bare stones, hanging on the tree. The birds had eaten the fruit. She and Jane and Melly had climbed up and had a good feast a week or two before, and Mrs Flower had picked all she could reach.

Polly jumped off the swing and ran to look at her

own garden. It was weedy and not very nice, but this was because it was not her best garden. Her best garden was at school, and she had spent all her time on it, and it was lovely. Polly felt excited when she thought of it, because she was almost sure that she and her friend Sara, who did the garden with her, were going to win the gardening prize. Tomorrow, at breaking-up, they would know.

She ran over to the garage, to fetch a fork to dig up the weeds in this garden. There was no motor-car in the garage yet. But there was everything else you can think of. There were the tools, and the hose, and the bulbs hanging up to dry and the sledge and everybody's bikes, and the wheelbarrow, and the plant pots, and the bit of canvas they used for a tent. Father used to say there was no room for a motor-car anyway so he had better not buy one.

There was also a huge tea-chest at one side which Polly had often meant to get into. She climbed in now, taking her doll with her. There was plenty of room in the tea-chest, and in the bottom were wood shavings which were as good as a cushion. On the top was a piece of canvas. She pulled this right over and covered the chest up.

She settled down inside, nursing the doll and pretending she was a proper mother. Like Aunt Caroline. They had been to see her in hospital, and there she lay, looking very pretty and frilly, with the baby in her arms. You were not allowed to breathe near the baby in case you gave it germs. She could not help breathing at Blackberry, because she was so close. Soon the tea-chest would be full of germs, and Polly thought it would be most unhealthy. But it did not matter as Blackberry was a doll, a black one. Really, she thought, this was more the kind of nest a cat would like, with all these shavings. It would be nice to be a mother cat, because the kittens were so furry, and you lick

them all over to keep them clean, which is less trouble than baths and soap and powder. She heard Jane and Melissa come in at the garage gate. The wheels of their bikes spun and made ticking noises. Polly hugged herself close and held her breath. She would not say she was there.

'I'm hungry,' said Jane.

'So am I,' said Melly. 'I'm dying to break-up.'

'I'm dying more for going away.'

'You can't die more.'

'Oh, come on. Leave the door.'

They went off over the lawn to the house. Polly laughed and kissed Blackberry. Everybody would wonder where she was. She would wait for her father and bounce out at him. It was cosy in the tea-chest, and she was comfortable. There was a tiny hole in the canvas and she could see a piece of blue sky through the garage door. She leaned her head back. She felt very sleepy. It was beastly about the pocket money. Perhaps Mummy would be sorry for her before the end of the window-paying. What could she make for Melly's birth-day . . .

At half past six Mrs Flower said to Melissa:

'Go and tell Polly to come, she's somewhere in

the garden. I haven't seen her for ages.'

So Melissa went.

'She isn't there, Mummy.'

'She must be, Melly. Look in the garage.'

Melissa went and looked again; but Polly was not there.

'I expect she's gone to the station, to meet Daddy. She ought to have told me.'

At seven o'clock Mr Flower arrived.

'Where's Polly?' said Mrs Flower.

'Polly?' said Mr Flower. 'Not in my pocket.'

'Didn't she come to meet you?'

'No,' he said.

'We don't know where she is,' said Mrs Flower. 'She's not in the house or garden.'

'She's gone to play with someone, I expect,' said their father.

Mrs Flower rang up all the places where Polly ever went to play. Polly was not at any of them.

'Mummy,' said Jane, 'do you think she could have gone up to the Hurst?'

'But she knows she's not allowed to go alone.'

'Shall Melly and I go and look for her?'

'No,' said their father. 'I'll go, on my bike. We don't want everyone getting lost.'

'The girls can go and look round the park, and I'll stay here in case she comes,' said their mother.

So Jane and Melly and Father all went to hunt for Polly.

In half an hour they were back again, but Polly was not with them.

'It's so late,' said Mrs Flower. 'This isn't like Polly.'

'Mummy, has she run away, do you think, because of the pebble and the window and all that?' Melly said.

'Oh no, I don't think so. Has either of you quarrelled with Polly?'

'No, not today,' said Jane. 'I've hardly seen her.'

Their father turned and went into the sitting-room and over to the telephone. Melissa and Jane followed.

'Mummy,' said Melly, running back in a minute. 'He's ringing up the police. Does he think Polly's been run over, Mummy?' And Melissa began to sniff.

Her mother comforted her.

'No, I don't think so for a moment,' she said. 'We shall find her soon. Now you and Jane come and have your supper, and go to bed. It's past your time.'

'I don't want any supper,' sobbed Melly, and even Jane looked pale and was very quiet, and said she felt sick.

'Jane, you look after Melly, and get quickly to bed.'

'They're doing all the routine things,' said their father.

'What are the routine things?' said Jane.

'Well, they'll find out if there's been an accident. And they'll get the police-cars out and search. They may even get the dogs out. They'll find her, anyway.'

And he went off on his bike again.

Jane and Melissa plodded slowly upstairs. Mrs Flower did not know what to do, she felt so worried. So she fetched some mending and did that. Every half-hour she went to the kitchen door, or to the front door, or into the garden, or into the road.

'Oh, where is she?' she thought.

And Mr Flower came back, without Polly.

Jane and Melly saw a police-car come, from Melly's window. The policeman spoke to their father and mother, but they could not hear what he said. Then the police-car drove off, and their father was in it.

Mrs Flower went back to the kitchen to wait. It was half past nine, but still not quite dark. Oh, where *was* Polly?

Then the kitchen door was pushed slowly open, and who should come in but Polly, as quiet as a mouse. She was blinking, and she had wood shavings in her hair, and her eyes looked dark.

'*Polly!*' said her mother, and she seized her and hugged her and could not help crying a few tears. 'Where have you been, darling?'

'I was in the tea-chest in the garage,' said Polly, feeling puzzled. 'I knew I must have been asleep, because when I was first there the sky was blue. And when I woke up it was nearly dark. Why are you crying, Mummy?'

'Because we thought you were lost,' said her mother, 'and I'm so glad to see you.'

'I thought people cried when they were sad,' Polly said, 'not glad.'

There was a stampede of slippery feet on the stairs. Jane and Melissa rushed in.

'Polly! Where have you been?' they said.

Melly's face was all smudged and dirty, like tears. And Jane's hair was twisted into corkscrews. She did it when she was worried. Polly felt very

warm inside, because everyone was so pleased to see her.

'You don't know what they're doing,' said Jane, feeling better. 'Police, and cars, and wireless and searchlights and dogs!'

'Oh, it's all right now,' said Mother, and she went straight to telephone the police.

Polly sat up that night, while the other two went to bed. She sat between her mother and father and had hot milk.

'Two late nights,' said Polly with glee, as she pushed off her pebble for Monday.

Down went another day on to the garden path.

4

Tuesday

'We're breaking-up, we're breaking-up,
 We're breaking-up, we're breaking-DOWN!'
Jane and Melly were doing the breaking-up game and the bedsprings were creaking. The game was to stand on your bed and jump, gently first, then higher and higher until you came to 'breaking-down', and then you flumped your whole body down on to the bed and bounced. It was lovely.

Polly scrambled up and began to do it, too.

'Hullo, Pie. You were lost last night,' called Jane.

'I know. We're breaking-up, we're breaking-up, we're breaking-up, we're breaking-DOWN,' Polly yelled.

'Hi! You young hooligans, stop it,' called Father from the bathroom. 'You'll ruin the springs. If you break your springs, I shall buy you all hammocks and you can sleep hung from the ceiling by two hooks.'

'Oh, *yes*,' said Jane. '*Do*, Daddy, it would be lovely. I shall break my springs on purpose. How would we climb in?'

'There'd have to be a ladder,' said Melissa, panting.

'You could swing in the hammock,' said Polly.

'It would hurt if you fell out of bed with a nightmare,' said Jane.

'Hooligans, hooligans, hooligans, hooligans,' muttered Polly, bouncing. It was a very good word to bounce to.

Outside school, Polly met Sara. They were both thinking the same thing.

'Let's just rush and see our garden,' Polly said,

'to make sure it's all right. I say, I got lost last night, they called the police.'

'You didn't!' said Sara. 'Where were you?'

'All the time I was asleep in the tea-chest in the garage. I felt queer when I woke up.'

They ran past the holm oak tree and past the netball courts to the part of the grounds where the gardens were. They were talking so hard about Polly being lost that they did not notice they had run past their garden. They ran back again. They could not find their garden. It looked different. Where was it? Which was it? It was this one, with the windy path. What had happened to it? They stood with their mouths open without saying a word.

There was not a single flower left, of all the flowers in their garden.

Sara went as pink as a rose. Polly's cheeks were as pale as a primrose. Her eyes filled with tears before she could stop them.

'Sara!'

'Who's done it?' Sara said. 'I'll kill them.'

'Oh,' Polly whispered, 'just when they were going to judge it. It was all ready. The beastly things,' she said.

'There are a few buds left,' said Sara. 'And there aren't any weeds, of course. It's all tidy. We might win for being tidy.'

But they had no hopes of this in their hearts. The garden had been full of flowers. Polly and Sara had bought plants with their pocket money, and they had grown seeds, too. Their fathers and grand-fathers had given them things. There were snap-dragons of every colour, pale poppies, penstem-mons, stocks, cornflowers, a foxglove, pansies,

pinks and a canterbury bell. Everybody had said how lovely it was. Sara and Polly had planned to pick them after breaking-up, and take half each.

'Fancy taking them all,' Sara said, sniffing.

'Oh, come on,' said Polly, rubbing her hand over her eyes. 'We'll be late.'

'Shall we report them?' Sara said jerkily, running along.

'I don't think it's much good now, do you?' Polly said, and Sara agreed.

Polly sat through breaking-up feeling very sad, and very sorry for herself. She was sad because she knew Jane and Melissa would have to go up to the platform, and she had thought that she would too for the garden prize. And now she could not possibly win that. It was so unfair. And this was why she felt sorry for herself. They had worked so hard, and she had told everyone that she would win. There was not time to find out who had done it, and make them own up, and alter the judging. Her eyes filled with tears again as she brooded on it.

Jane went up for her music certificate. Melissa went up for her junior games badge. The head-mistress went on and on reading out the lists. The gardening prize came last of all. Sara and Polly looked at the floor in front of their crossed legs, and went very red, and nudged each other.

'Polly Flower, what a suitable name,' said the head-mistress, 'and Sara James. A beautiful garden, which has given pleasure to us all.'

Polly looked at Sara, and Sara looked at Polly, with their mouths wide open again and the tears still in their eyes. This would not do.

'Come on,' whispered Polly, and she blew her nose and led the way.

The prize was a new set of garden tools each, shiny and sharp. Polly's was green, and Sara's was red. There were also some packets of seeds. The head-mistress told them how hard they had worked, which they knew, and everybody clapped, and that was that. Polly and Sara could not understand it.

But when Polly got home and showed her mother the tools, Mrs Flower explained it quite simply.

'I expect they judged them at the week-end, darling,' she said. 'I wonder who took the flowers, though?'

Melissa got up and ran off into the garden.

'Now, Pie. Now she's gone, I've had an idea what you can make for her birthday.'

'Oh, what?' said Polly.

'Toffee!' said Mrs Flower. 'We'll do it this afternoon, while Jane and Melly have gone to Caroline's for me.'

'Yes,' Polly said. 'Can I make lots? She'll love it.'

Polly set to work. She put on her red-checked apron. She got the pan and the wooden spoon, and the brown sugar and the treacle. She had made toffee before, she was good at it. But this was extra-super toffee, with butter, not margarine. She greased the tin to have it all ready. She was very hot, stirring the toffee over the gas-ring. When it had bubbled long enough, she took it off and poured it out. The toffee spread in a thick, golden-brown, bubbly coil into the greased tin, pushing the grease in front of it.

'Isn't it gorgeous? Won't she love it, Mummy? Do you think it will be her best present?' Polly said.

She could hardly wait for the toffee to set. Meanwhile she found a tin with a picture of horses and foals on it, which she thought Melly would like. She lined it with some crinkly paper. When the toffee was set, she tapped it smartly with the little hammer. It broke into dozens of exciting jagged pieces. (It reminded her a bit of her window.)

'It's perfect,' said her mother. The tin was

hardly big enough for all the pieces. Polly let herself have a few splinters, and her mother tasted it too. Then she carried the tin up to her bedroom, tied a ribbon and a message on it, and put it under her bed.

Polly had to go to bed early that night. She pushed off Tuesday, thinking that it had been a lovely day. The gardening prize, and the toffee. Clink, fell Tuesday's pebble against another on the path.

Only three more days! She lay in bed, and although the curtains were drawn it was still quite light. She could hear cars, and people down the road. She could hear Jane's lovely practice begin. She was too hot. Oh dear, she could not go to sleep. Then she thought of the toffee, sitting there under her bed, ready to put by Melly's plate in the morning.

She was sure one piece would not show, and it was just what she wanted. She leaned over, untied the ribbon, opened the tin, and took a large, jagged piece of toffee.

'Oh, it's deluscious.' (This meant half luscious and half delicious, and was Polly's own word.)

When she had sucked it, she could not help having another piece. She only had to put her arm down. She was sure a few pieces would make no difference, because the tin was too full, anyway. She was sorry about her teeth, but then the harm was done now. She could not creep and clean them again without someone hearing. So she went on sucking and chewing and crunching and gulping. She could not help herself. Now the tin felt rather empty to her fingers. She really must not eat any more after this last piece. She must close it up. Perhaps it would not look so empty as it felt. She hoped not.

5

Wednesday

Polly woke up early on Wednesday morning. First she remembered it was Melly's birthday. Then she remembered the toffee. She leaned over the side of the bed and pulled out the tin. She opened it. It was not even half full. In places you could see the paper on the bottom. Polly shook it miserably. But however much she did this, the toffee grew no more. How could she have eaten Melly's toffee? She wished very hard that she had not been so greedy. Would it be better not to give it to her at all? But then she had nothing else to give her, and no time to make another present.

As it was, the Flower family only liked some kinds of home-made presents. If you gave somebody a home-made present just so that you need not spend your own pocket money, you were thought mean. But what if you made it, and then could not stop yourself eating it? . . . Polly was ashamed. She felt like rushing in to tell Melly, giving her what was left, and asking her not to show anybody. But this seemed cowardly. And at this moment, Jane called out:

'Many happy returns of the day, Melly!'

So Polly shut the tin, and tied on the bow and the label quickly.

'Many happy returns of the day, Melly!' she said, not so loudly.

'Thank you,' said Melly, in a pleased voice. No school, her birthday, and she was ten.

'I'm ten,' she said, 'exactly.'

'You'll never be as old as I am,' said Jane.

'Yes, I shall, in two years I'll be twelve.'

'By that time I'll be fourteen.'

'You mean, I'll never catch you up.'

'When Jane's eighty,' said Polly, 'Melly will be seventy-eight, and I shall be seventy-six.'

'Goodness,' said Melly, and scrambled into her clothes.

By Melissa's plate and on her chair, the presents were piled, strange, brown-paper shapes, making you try to guess what they were. How lovely to be Melissa, Polly thought. She could not help wishing it were her birthday. But then it would be nice to see Melissa being pleased. She added her tin to the pile, down by the chair leg, when no one was

looking. Then she ran out to the kitchen.

Birthday people could choose their food. Melissa had chosen grapefruit and grilled kippers. The smell of the kippers made Polly feel that she could eat six. When breakfast was ready and everybody was there, Melly began unwrapping her presents. There was a long present looking like a huge brown-paper spoon. It was a tennis racquet from her father! Melly's eyes shone at him. She had just begun to learn properly. There were six white, new balls in a string net from Grandpa, to play with.

'Oh, Jane! We'll be able to play on the park courts,' Melly said.

'Yes,' said Jane, 'and Polly can be ball-boy.'

There was a kite from her mother, to fly at the sea. There was a great, long present from Aunt Caroline which looked as if it must be a broom, but turned into a superb shrimping-net. There was a new leather purse with two new 50p pieces in it from Uncle Peter. From Grandma there was a work-box, with a needle-case made of scarlet silk and a silver thimble with a border of painted flowers, which Grandma had used when she was Melissa's age. From Jane there was a small, grey velvet mole to add to Melly's collection of animals, and a pair of treacle-tin stilts, which Jane had made. She had enamelled the tins bright green, taken off their lids and made two holes in the bottom, one each side, by hammering a skewer through. Through the holes she threaded a strong string. You stood on the tins, held the string handles, and ran as fast as you could. On the pavement it sounded like a horse coming. Melly unpacked, and thanked and gasped, and jumped up and down until the floor was smothered in paper and string and presents. At last she dived down and brought up Polly's tin.

'Oh, and there's this!' she said.

Polly began to chew her toast very hard. She felt as if her kipper were going to choke her.

'Toffee! Yum, yum. Thank you, Polly, did you make it?'

'Yes,' Polly muttered.

'Have a piece, Mummy?' Melly said.

'Not with my kipper,' said Mrs Flower, laughing. But she looked at the open tin.

And then she looked at Polly.

'Polly!' she said rather softly, in her voice that sounded half-amused and half-ashamed of you. And she looked back at the tin.

'Why, what?' Jane said, looking too. 'Has she gone and eaten some? I bet it ought to be full.'

Polly felt herself going pink. But her mother did not tell. She looked at her mother anxiously. Then she looked at her father, who was looking at her mother. Then she looked at Melly who for once was allowed to eat toffee in the middle of breakfast, and was choosing a piece.

'It's heavenly,' she said. 'Anyway, there's quite a lot.'

'I *did* eat some,' Polly confessed. 'I'll make some more for you, Melly.'

'No, you needn't, because . . .' Melly began. And she suddenly went bright red, and stopped.

'Because what?' Jane said. 'Why are both my little sisters blushing like beetroots?' Jane spoke like this when she felt grown-up.

'Because I think I know who took Polly's and Sara's flowers, and I didn't say,' Melissa blurted.

'Oh, do you, darling. Who?' asked Mrs Flower.

'Well, you know that girl, Carol Robins?'

'I should think I do know her,' said Jane.

'She asked me if she could pick just one or two of Polly's flowers, and I said yes. I know I ought to have made her ask you, Polly. But I knew they'd done the judging. And I thought one or two wouldn't show. And I think she must have picked the whole lot. She wanted them for Miss Bates.'

'So that's where those flowers in the music room came from!' Jane said. 'A simply enormous bunch, and Batey told me Carol had brought them from her garden at home!'

'And they were mine,' said Polly. 'Mine and Sara's. She is a fibber!'

'I don't suppose she actually said it. She let Batey think so. She's always bringing flowers, because she can't do her chromatic scales, she thinks it does instead. You ought to have told *me*, Melly, I'd have knocked her down!' Jane said fiercely.

'*I* think,' said Mr Flower, standing up to go to work, 'I think Melissa and Polly are now quits.'

'Yes, so do I,' said their mother.

'How much did you eat?' Jane said. 'Was the tin full? You could be sick, you know.'

'Don't go on, Jane. I seem to remember somebody who ate a whole plate of brandy snaps before tea began once.'

Everybody laughed at Jane, including Jane.

Polly felt glad the toffee business was over, in a

(130)

better way than she deserved, so that she could enjoy the rest of Melly's birthday. Six people came to tea, enough to do the sports Jane had arranged. A sack race, an obstacle race, a plant-pot race, a hopping race, a skipping race, a jumping race, and a slow-bicycle race, with 10p pieces for prizes. Polly won the sack race, and gave her 10p to Melly, to make up for the toffee.

'Only two more days,' she said to herself that night. Whish went Wednesday, and lay shining up at her from the path.

6

Thursday

Thursday was hot and beautiful. Polly tried to outstare the sun, as he shone through her window. It was mended now.

'This time tomorrow!' sang Melissa.

'We shall still be precisely here,' said Jane.

'How long can you stare at the sun for?' Polly asked them. 'Without shutting your eyes? Count.'

'It's bad for your eyes,' Jane said. 'I bet you don't know how far away the sun is, Pie.'

'A thousand miles?' said Polly, blinking.

'A million miles?' called Melissa.

'Ninety-three million miles!' announced Jane, with awe.

'Goodness!' Melly said, and bounced out of bed.

All the week they had not been able to wear this, that and the next thing because it was being kept clean for the holiday. Or it was being washed or ironed ready to go. Today was even worse, for Mrs Flower was going to pack the trunk. Father had 'broken-up' from work, and he was standing at the garden-table in the sun, polishing all the shoes.

Mother was kneeling by the big, white leather trunk, calling out each layer as she wanted it. Jane, Melissa and Polly were the fetchers and carriers.

'All the hard things first. Only two books each,' said Mrs Flower. 'Everybody fetch her spare shoes from Daddy and stuff them with socks.'

Melissa arrived back with her new shrimping-net as well as her shoes.

'Corner to corner, Mummy,' she said.

'No, Melly, it won't: you'll have to carry it. I only hope you won't blind anybody. Yes, you can put the kite in.'

'Mummy, if Melly's having the kite, can I put Blackberry in?' said Polly.

'Yes, you may. Daddy's paints, Jane's camera, my writing things. Bathing suits and towels. Underclothes. Polly, fetch me a pile you'll see in the airing cupboard, right in front. And Polly, why are you wearing that dress? That's the dress you've got to travel in.'

'Because everything else is in,' Polly said.

'Mummy, you've forgotten all the spades!' sang Jane.

'You mean you've forgotten them,' said Mrs Flower, and she stuffed them down the sides. 'You should be in your oldest shorts and shirt, Polly.'

'But I hate them,' said Polly.

'If you get the dress dirty, there'll be no time to wash and iron it,' said her mother.

'I *promise* I won't get it dirty,' Polly said.

'I think you're a silly girl, but I haven't time to argue,' said her mother. 'Fetch me your blazers and cardigans, everybody, and your shorts. And then all the blouses.'

In they all went, the tee shirts and sundresses, pyjamas and nightdresses and handkerchiefs. Polly suddenly thought of Blackberry shut in the trunk all night and all the next day and did not like it. She went and burrowed and pulled her out by her black curls.

'She'll smother,' she said. 'She can go in my little case.'

And at last it was done and Mr Flower sat on it and locked it and strapped it, and Jane wrote the labels in her good round writing. After lunch Mrs Flower heaved a big long sigh and said:

'Now, I shall have a lovely rest in the hair-dresser's.'

And away she went.

Jane was helping her father mow the lawn, the

last cut it would get for a month. Melissa sat in a deck-chair sewing, with her new work-basket beside her and her silver thimble on her finger. Polly said:

'Melly, can I have a go on your treacle-tin stilts?'

'Yes,' said Melly.

So Polly balanced herself on the treacle-tins, and held the strings and off she went, clomp, clomp, trying to keep up with her father and the mowing machine. Then she thought it might be easier on the pavement, so she went out of the garage gate to try.

Clomp, clomp, clomp, clomp.

The pavement was very smooth. Little by little Polly began to go faster.

Clompty, clompty, clompty, clompty, clomp. She thought she might try running now, as Jane did. It was fun, she liked doing it.

Clompety, clompety, clompety, clompety, clompety, crash wallop went the stilts as if they were running away from her, and over she went, thump, on to the pavement. The pavement was only hard and smooth, but her hand went against the fence and grazed itself and started to bleed.

'Hurt yourself, Pie?' said her father.

'Only this hand. Daddy, I *nearly* ran!'

'Go and wash it and bring the iodine,' he said.

So Polly did. She stood on the bathroom box to reach the medicine chest. She saw the iodine, and took hold of it. Somebody had left the cork not properly in. As Polly tipped the bottle of iodine the cork came out and a great brown stream went all down the front of her dress. Her dress! Which Mummy had told her to change! Which she had to go away in! Oh, help! She left the bottle, and ran madly down to her father.

'Daddy! Daddy! Look what's happened! My dress. It wasn't my fault, the cork wasn't in, it tipped all over me——'

'Good gracious, child, quick, up to the bathroom, and get it off. Hurry, I'm coming,' said her father, and he left the mower, and dashed after Polly, and Jane left the barrow, and Melly left her sewing, and they all ran up to see. Father brought a bottle (Polly never knew what was in it). He turned on the cold tap and he plunged the dress into the bath, and put some of the stuff from the bottle in the water. And all the horrible brown stain ran out of the dress! Like magic! Father swilled and swished the dress, until there was no stain left at all. Polly felt so grateful, she hugged him as he knelt by the bath. This was just like Father. He always knew what to do, and he always did it quickly. He did not stand about deciding. Once, Jane had left her bunch of wild daffodils on a bus. She screamed: 'My daffodils!' because she wanted them so badly. She loved them and had never picked them before. So Father had rushed in front of the bus and waved his arms, laughing, and the bus stopped at once, and Jane had found her daffodils. (Jane was like Father herself, and always did things quickly.)

'Well!' he said. 'What a kettle-of-fish, as Grandma would say.'

'Daddy, I've got to wear it tomorrow. Mummy told me to change and I——'

'We'll get it dry, it's hot.'

'Will you be able to iron it? Before Mummy comes back?'

'Oh, I daresay,' said Father airily. He did not care for ironing.

'I'll iron it!' offered Jane.

'Oh, thank you, Jane.'

'Come on, wring it out,' said Melly. 'I'll go and put the line up and get the pegs. We can keep it a secret, it'll be fun.'

So they hung it up in the hot sun. Polly could do nothing but go and feel it all the afternoon, and ask her father the time. She felt she must have it hanging in her cupboard, and ready to wear before her mother came home.

At last Jane said it was dry enough to iron, and Father looked at his watch and said:

'You'll have to get cracking, Jane.'

'Oh, quick, quick,' pleaded Polly.

Jane rushed into the kitchen and put up the ironing-board. Melissa got the iron and plugged it in. What a long time it seemed to take, getting hot! Polly danced from toe to toe. Jane held up the iron and tried it with a wet finger. Psst! It was ready. Jane began to iron Polly's dress, up and down the skirt, over the board.

'Good job there aren't any sleeves much, or pleats. I hate pleats,' said Jane.

'It's a good thing Mummy was having her hair waved, is all I can say,' said Father.

Jane ironed and ironed, the bodice, and between the buttons, and the collar.

'She's coming, she's coming!' yelled Melly from the dining-room window.

'It's all right. It's done!' said Jane. 'Nobody say a word!'

And Polly ran up the stairs with the dress, just as Mrs Flower's key went click in the lock. Father was very sly.

'How lovely you look,' he said, and he held on to Mother, looking at her hair, before he kissed her, so that Jane had time to put the board away, and Melly had time to undo the iron, and Polly had time to hang up the dress.

They had tea under the cherry tree.

'I see Polly has had the sense to change her dress,' remarked Mrs Flower.

Father laughed. Polly went pink. Jane made a screwy face with her mouth twisted. Melly choked in her tea and started to laugh.

So in the end, they had to tell Mrs Flower all about it.

That night when Polly had pushed off her pebble, there was only one left.

'Tomorrow!' she said to her mother. And thump fell Thursday, the sixth white pebble.

'This time tomorrow, Melly!' she squealed.

'I know,' Melly said, coming up to bed.

The grass smelt lovely where Father had mowed it. From the drawing-room door, which opened into the garden, Polly could hear Jane's practice begin. She jumped into bed and hung on to her mother so hard that her mother had to tickle Polly to get herself loose.

7

Friday

Before she was properly awake, Polly knew that something wonderful was going to happen on Friday. Then she remembered. They were going away to the sea!

She was so excited that she could hardly eat any breakfast. At last they were ready to go. The windows were fastened and the doors were locked, except for the front one: and everybody's little case stood ready in the hall, and the trunk stood ready in the porch waiting for the taxi to take them all to the station.

Suddenly Father put his hand into his inside breast pocket, and took out his crocodile notecase. He opened it. He put his hand into all his other pockets. Then he clapped his hand to his head, and said, very loudly, like an actor:

'Stop! I've lost the tickets!'

Polly gazed at her father, as if she were frozen.

Father, who could run in front of buses and get iodine out of dresses! Could he really have lost the tickets? It was astonishing but it seemed to be true.

'Daddy, you're teasing,' said Jane.

'Charles, you couldn't,' said Mother.

'Shan't we be able to go?' whispered Melly.

And Polly said nothing.

'Were they in the notecase?' said Mother.

'No, they were in the envelope with the booked seats for the train,' said Father. 'The envelope was with the notecase. And now it isn't. Someone has spirited it away. Everybody search the house for a buff-coloured envelope,' ordered Father, and he ran up the stairs three at a time.

'What's buff?' said Polly.

'Fawn,' said Mother.

'I must have put it down somewhere,' called Father. 'I don't remember seeing it, I thought it was with my notecase, of course.'

Everybody looked everywhere. They looked in the dining-room and in the sitting-room and in the kitchen and by the telephone and in the hall and on the stairs and in all the bedrooms. Jane looked behind the clock. Father looked in his desk, and Mother looked in hers, and even in the kitchen drawers amongst the tea-towels. Polly looked under her bed. She had said good-bye to her room once, and now she had to creep in without noticing it, and not wake it up. But how could a buff envelope have got under her bed? It had not.

When Mother packed the trunk, she had sent Polly for Daddy's sports coat. It was in the garden, with him, on the table, because he had been too hot. He had taken the things out of the pockets and given it to Polly. Polly shut her door and bolted down the stairs.

'Daddy! You might have left it in the coat Mummy packed yesterday!' she explained. 'You took the things out, you might have not taken them all out!'

Father stopped dead in the hall.

'Thoughtful and intelligent child!' he said. 'Quick, the trunk.'

The taxi slid up to the front gate.

'The taxi's here!' said Melly.

'You go and keep him busy with your shrimping-net,' ordered Father. And he dived for the trunk, undid the straps, undid the lock (he had the keys in his pocket), threw up the lid, and found his coat. It was near the top, which was lucky. Father felt in

the breast pocket. His eyebrows went up in the way they did, and his mouth curled. Polly watched. She saw him pull out a buff-coloured envelope!

'Three cheers for Polly,' said Father softly, winking at her.

'Thank goodness,' said Mother.

'Thank heavens,' said Jane.

But Melissa was watching the taxi-man.

'Is it safe on top?' she said. 'It's my shrimping-net and I only had it the day before yesterday.'

'Look, I've wedged it, see?' said the man. 'But if you cares to sit on top wiv it, you're welcome. Morning, Ma'am,' he went on, '\'aven't you forgot the spades and pails and the water-wings and the li-lo and the beach-hut?'

And he did not laugh at all, and Polly thought he was angry for being kept waiting. But when Mother laughed, he rubbed his hands and looked pleased with himself. This is the way taxi-men often talk near London. They are not cross, they are only trying to make you laugh.

And this was only the beginning. For first they had to catch the train into London. And then they had to have another taxi from Victoria to Liverpool Street. And then they had to catch the main train.

And every time there were three children, with three small cases, one hand-case for Father, travelling-bag for Mother, white leather trunk, and the shrimping-net. Mrs Flower stood counting them all at each change.

The main train was very long indeed. Father gave the booked-seat tickets to Jane, and Jane strode up the platform followed by Melly and the shrimping-net, Polly and her case, and Mother and the travelling-bag, looking for the carriage where they were to sit. Meanwhile Father and a porter saw to the trunk.

But then they were all safely in the carriage, with the cases and coats on the rack, and the shrimping-net wedged beneath them! Then, Polly thought,

the holiday had really begun. She gazed out of the window, too excited to speak. She loved swaying along the corridor to the dining-car to have lunch on the train. She loved watching the town turn into country. Some of the fields were harvested already, and the barley stood in shaggy, pointed houses, each with its own shadow. She loved breathing on the window and drawing faces. Or playing noughts-and-crosses with Melly. Or sitting next to Father, who could draw funny pictures. Or even just thinking. She thought of her room at home. Suddenly she thought of the seventh white pebble! Today's pebble.

'Mummy!'

'Yes?'

'I didn't push today's pebble off!' said Polly.

'I'm afraid you can't go back now,' said Father.

'You should have shoved it off last night,' said Jane.

'I couldn't, because it wasn't today yet.'

'You should have pushed it off this morning,' said Melly.

'Isn't it funny to think of it sitting there on its own, and us being so far away,' Polly said.

'Most strange,' said her mother.

'It's like, "where's yesterday today", isn't it?'

'Rather the same,' said her father.

Meanwhile, there they all were in the railway carriage, hurrying over the one hundred and sixty miles of the journey. Father was thinking what strange things Polly said, and how good it was to have time to sit back and read his book. Mother was thinking how rich it made her feel to have all her family so close around her that she could look at them each in turn. She wondered what her children would do when they grew up: Jane and Melissa and Polly, each so different. They would grow up and be ready to leave their family, which was like this comfortable railway carriage where they all travelled together. They would get out, and do different things on their own. She was wishing life could always be happy and lovely for them and that she could protect them from sad and horrid things. (Mothers always wish this but they know it is no use, because life is a mixture of sad and happy things, and everybody has to have a share of both.)

Jane was reading her book and sucking a sweet. Melissa was swinging her legs and longing to practise her diving, from the green sea-weeded breakwater into the green curling sea. Ti tiddelly tum, ti tiddelly tum, ti tiddelly tum, went the train as if it were pleased to be taking people to the sea. And Polly was gazing out at the rushing, flying country: trees and fields and houses and haystacks and cows and horses and level-crossings and people, and thinking what hundreds of millions of different things there were in this round, interesting world.